Cockfight

MARÍA FERNANDA AMPUERO

Translated from the Spanish by **Frances Riddle**

THE FEMINIST PRESS
AT THE CITY UNIVERSITY OF NEW YORK
NEW YORK CITY

Published in 2020 by the Feminist Press
at the City University of New York
The Graduate Center
365 Fifth Avenue, Suite 5406
New York, NY 10016

feministpress.org

First Feminist Press edition 2020

 This book is supported in part by an award from the
National Endowment for the Arts.

 This book was made possible thanks to a grant from
New York State Council on the Arts with the support of
Governor Andrew M. Cuomo and the New York State
Legislature.

First printing May 2020

Cover design by Sukruti Anah Staneley
Text design by Drew Stevens

Library of Congress Cataloging-in-Publication Data
Names: Ampuero, María Fernanda, author. | Riddle, Frances, translator.
Title: Cockfight / María Fernanda Ampuero ; translated from the Spanish by
    Frances Riddle.
Description: First Feminist Press edition. | New York, NY : The Feminist
    Press, 2020. | Translated into English from Spanish.
Identifiers: LCCN 2019035462 (print) | LCCN 2019035463 (ebook) | ISBN
    9781936932825 (paperback) | ISBN 9781936932832 (epub)
Subjects: LCSH: Ampuero, María Fernanda--Translations into English.
Classification: LCC PQ8220.41.M68 A2 2020 (print) | LCC PQ8220.41.M68
    (ebook) | DDC 863/.7--dc23
LC record available at https://lccn.loc.gov/2019035462
LC ebook record available at https://lccn.loc.gov/2019035463

PRINTED IN THE UNITED STATES OF AMERICA

CONTENTS

Everything that rots forms a family.
—FABIÁN CASAS

Am I a monster or is this what it means to be human?
—CLARICE LISPECTOR,
translated by Giovanni Pontiero

AUCTION

There are roosters around here somewhere.

Kneeling, with my head down and covered by a filthy rag, I concentrate on hearing them: how many there are, if they're in cages or inside a pen. When I was young, my dad raised gamecocks, and since there wasn't anyone else to look after me, he'd take me along to the fights. The first few times, I cried when I saw the poor rooster ripped to shreds in the sand, and he laughed and called me a girl.

At night, giant vampire roosters devoured my insides. I would scream and he'd come running to my bed, and again he'd call me a girl.

"Come on, don't be such a girl. They're just roosters, dammit."

Eventually I stopped crying when I saw the hot guts of the losing rooster in the dust. I was the one who had to clean up the ball of feathers and viscera and carry it all to the trash bin. I would say: "Bye-bye, rooster. Be happy in heaven where there are thousands of worms and fields and corn and families that love roosters." On the way, some cockfighter would give me a piece of candy or a coin to touch me or kiss me, or for me to touch him or kiss him. I was afraid that if I told Dad, he'd call me a girl again.

"Come on, don't be such a girl. They're just cockfighters, dammit."

One night, a rooster's belly exploded as I was carrying it in my arms like a doll, and I discovered that those macho men who shouted and jeered for one rooster to rip open the other were disgusted by the shit and blood and guts of the dead rooster. So I covered my hands, my knees, and my face with that mixture, and they didn't bother me with kisses and all that bullshit anymore.

They said to my dad, "Your daughter is a monster."

And he responded that they were the monsters and they clinked their shot glasses.

"You guys are the monsters. Salud."

The smell inside the cockpit was disgusting. Sometimes when I fell asleep in a corner, under the stands, I'd wake up with one of those men peeking underneath my school uniform at my underwear. So before falling asleep I would stick a rooster head between my legs. One, sometimes more. A whole belt of rooster heads. Those macho guys didn't like lifting up a skirt to find little severed heads.

Sometimes, Dad would wake me up to clear away a gutted rooster. Sometimes, he did the cleaning himself, and his friends called him a faggot, asked him why the hell he even bothered to bring his daughter. He just gathered up the ruined and bloody rooster. Then from the door he blew them a kiss. His friends laughed.

I know that here, somewhere, there are roosters because I'd recognize that smell from a thousand miles away. The smell of my life, the smell of my father. It smells of blood, of man, of shit, of cheap liquor, of sour sweat and industrial grease. You don't exactly have to be a genius to gather that this is some abandoned place, hidden away god knows where, and that I'm totally fucked.

A man speaks. He must be around forty. I imagine him fat, bald, and dirty, wearing a sleeveless white undershirt, shorts, and flip-flops; I imagine his pinkie and thumb nails are long. I can tell by the way he's speaking that there are other people here. There's someone else here besides me. There are other people on their knees, with their heads bent, covered by dark, disgusting sacks.

"Come on now, let's all calm down—the first *sonofabitch* who makes a sound is gonna get a bullet in his head. If you all cooperate, we'll all make it through the night in one piece."

I feel his stomach brush against my head and then the barrel of a gun. No, he's not joking.

A girl cries a few feet to my right. I suppose she couldn't handle the feeling of the gun to her temple. The sound of a slap.

"Look, princess. No crying, you hear me? Or are you in a big hurry to meet your maker?"

Later, the fat man with the gun walks away. He's gone to talk on the phone. He says a number: "Six, six motherfuckers." He also says, "It's a good haul, really good, the best in months." He says they won't want to miss it. He makes one call after another. He forgets, for a while, about us.

Beside me I hear a cough muffled by a hood, a man's cough.

"I've heard about this," he says, very softly. "I thought it was a myth, an urban legend. They're called auctions. Taxi drivers choose passengers they think they'll be able to get good money for and they kidnap them. Then buyers come and bid on their favorites. And they take them. They keep their things, they force them to steal, to open up their houses, to give them their credit card numbers. And the women . . . the women."

"What?" I ask.

He hears that I'm a woman. He goes quiet.

The first thing I thought when I got in the taxi that night was *finally*. I rested my head on the seat and closed my eyes. I'd had several drinks and I was depressed. I'd been at the bar with a man I pretended to be friends with. With him and his wife. I always pretend, I'm good at pretending. But when I got in the taxi, I sighed and said to myself, "What a relief: now I can go home and cry myself to sleep." I think I dozed off for a minute, and suddenly, when I opened my eyes, I was in an unfamiliar place. An industrial area. Empty. Darkness. Mind-numbing fear: someone was about to fuck up my life forever.

The taxi driver pulled out a gun, looked me in the eye, and said with absurd politeness: "We've reached your destination, miss."

What followed was quick. Someone opened the door before I could lock it and put a sack over my head, they tied my hands, shoved me into this sort of garage that smelled like a rotting cockpit, and made me kneel in a corner.

The sound of conversations. The fat man and someone else and then someone else and someone else. People keep coming. The sound of laughter and beers being opened. The scent of weed and some other shit with a spicy smell. The man next to me finally stops telling me to keep calm. He must be saying it to himself now.

He mentioned before that he has an eight-month-old baby and a three-year-old son. He must be thinking about them. And about these junkies getting inside the gated community where they live. That must be what he's thinking about. About waving to the guard to open the gate while these beasts duck down in the back seat. He's going to take them home to meet his beautiful wife, his eight-month-old baby, and his three-year-old son. He's going to take them to his house.

And there's nothing he can do about it.

Farther away, to the right, murmuring, a girl cries, I don't know if it's the same one who was crying before. The fat man fires his gun and we all drop to the floor. He hasn't shot us, he's just shot. It doesn't matter, the terror has ripped us in half. He and his friends laugh. They come over, they move us into the center of the room.

"All right, gentlemen, ladies, tonight's auction is officially open. They're all so lovely, so well-behaved. Now, you stand here for me. Closer, princess. Riiiiight there. Don't be afraid, little lady, I don't bite.

Just like that. So these gentlemen can decide which one of you they're going to take. The rules are the same as always, gentlemen: the most money gets the best prize. If you could leave your guns over here for me, I'll keep them safe till the auction's over. Thank you. Delighted, as always, to have you."

The fat man presents us like he's hosting a TV show. We can't see the audience, but we know the men who are looking at us, sizing us up, are thieves. And rapists. They are definitely rapists. And murderers. They might be murderers. Or something worse.

"Laaaaaadies and geeeeeeentlemen!"

The fat man doesn't like the ones who whimper or the ones who say they have kids or the ones who shout desperately, "You don't know who you're messing with!" No. He likes even less the ones who say he's going to rot in jail. All these people, men and women alike, have been punched in the gut. I've heard them fall to the floor breathless. I focus on the roosters. Maybe there aren't any. But I hear them. Inside me. Men and roosters. *Come on, don't be such a girl. They're just cock-fighters, dammit.*

"This man, what's our first participant's name? What? Speak up, friend. Ricardooooo, welcoooome. He wears a nice watch and some niiiiice Adidas shoes. Ricardoooo must have moneyyyyyyyy! Let's take a look at Ricardo's wallet. Credit cards, ohhhhhh a Visa *Goooaaald* by Messi."

The fat man tells bad jokes.

They start to bid on Ricardo. Someone offers three hundred, another person eight hundred. The fat man adds that Ricardo lives in a gated community outside the city: Riverview.

"A view poor folks like us can't even get a glimpse of. That's where our friend Richie lives. You don't mind if we call you Richie, do you? Like Richie Rich."

A terrifying voice says five thousand. The terrifying voice takes Ricardo away. The others applaud.

"Sold to the man with the mustache for five thousand!"

The fat man fondles Nancy, a girl who speaks with a thread of a voice. I know he's groping her because he says, "Look at these delicious tits, such perky nipples," and he sucks up his drool and says things you don't say without touching and, also, who's to stop him from touching her? No one. Nancy sounds young. Early twenties. She could be a nurse or a schoolteacher. The fat man starts to undress Nancy. We hear him unbuckle her belt and unbutton her jeans and rip her underwear while she says *please* so many times and with such fear in her voice that we all stain our filthy hoods with tears. "Look at this fine little ass. What a beauty." He licks Nancy, Nancy's ass. We hear the sound. The men jeer, roar, applaud. Then the slap of flesh against flesh. And the howls. The howls.

"Gentlemen, just some quality control for you. I give her a ten. You can clean her up real pretty and our friend Nancy will be a delight."

She must be beautiful because they bid, immediately, two thousand, three thousand, three thousand five. Nancy goes for three thousand five. Sexy goes for less than wealthy.

"And the lucky man taking this lovely piece of ass home is the gentleman with the gold ring and the cross!"

We're sold off one by one. The fat man manages to get a lot of information out of the guy next to me, the one with the eight-month-old baby and the three-year-old son, and now he's the auction's prized pig: money in different accounts, high-up executive, son of a businessman, art collector, kids, wife. The guy is a winning lottery ticket. They'll probably ask ransom for him. The bid starts at five thousand. It goes up to ten, fifteen. It stops at twenty. Someone intimidating has offered twenty thousand. A new voice. He's come just for this. He wasn't interested in wasting his time on anyone else.

The fat man doesn't make any jokes.

When it's my turn I think about the roosters. I close my eyes and open my sphincter. I know that this is the most important thing I will do in my life, so I do it right. I soak my legs, my feet, the floor. I'm in the center of a room, surrounded by criminals, displayed before them like cattle, and like cattle I empty my bowels. As best I can, I rub one leg against the other, I assume the position of a gutted doll. I scream like a madwoman. I shake my head, mutter obscenities, gibberish, the things I used to say to the roosters about a heaven filled with endless corn and worms. I know the fat man is about to shoot me.

But instead, he busts my lip open with his hand. I bite my tongue. The blood drips onto my chest, down my belly, mixes with the shit and piss. I start to laugh, deranged, to laugh, and laugh, and laugh.

He doesn't know what to do.

"How much for this monster?"

No one wants to bid.

The fat man offers up my watch, my cell phone, my purse. They're all cheap, made in China. He grabs my tits in an attempt to encourage them and I shriek.

"Fifteen, twenty?"

But nothing, no one.

They toss me outside. They hose me down and then they put me in a car that leaves me wet, barefoot, dazed, on the side of the highway.

MONSTERS

Narcisa used to say that we should be more afraid of the living than the dead, but we didn't believe her because in all the horror movies we saw, we were most afraid of the dead, the ones that had returned from beyond, the possessed. Mercedes was terrified of demons and I was terrified of vampires. We talked about it all the time. About satanic possessions and about men with fangs who fed on the blood of little girls. Mom and Dad bought us dolls and books of fairy tales, and we reenacted *The Exorcist* with the dolls and made believe that Prince Charming was really a vampire who woke Snow White up to turn her undead. During the day everything was fine, we were brave, but at night we always asked Narcisa to stay upstairs with us. Dad didn't like Narcisa sleeping in our room—he called her *the help*—but it was inevitable: we told her that if she didn't come up, we'd go down to sleep with *the help* in her room. That seemed to terrify her. And so Narcisa, who must've been about fourteen years old, tried to protest, saying that she didn't want to sleep with us, that we should be more afraid of the living than the dead.

And we thought it was ridiculous because how could anyone be more afraid of Narcisa, for example, than of Regan, the girl from *The Exorcist*, or more afraid of Don Pepe the gardener than of the Salem vampires or of Damien, the Antichrist, or more afraid of Dad than of the Wolf Man. Absurd.

Mom and Dad were never home—Dad worked and Mom played bridge with neighbors—that's why Mercedes and I could go rent horror movies at the video store every day after school. The boy who worked there never said a word to us. We knew that the cases said over sixteen or eighteen, but the boy never said anything. His face was covered in zits and he was fat, he always had a fan pointing at his crotch. The only time he ever talked to us was when we rented *The Shining*. He looked at it, then looked at us, and said:

"There are some girls just like you in this. Both of them are dead, their dad killed them."

Mercedes grabbed my hand. And we stood there like that, holding hands, in our matching uniforms, staring at him until he gave us the movie.

Mercedes was a big scaredy-cat. Pale, sickly. Mom said that I must've eaten up everything that came down the umbilical cord because she was tiny when she was born, a little worm, and I, on the other hand, was born like a bull. That's the word everyone used: *bull*. And the bull had to take care of the worm, who else would? Sometimes I wished I could be the worm, but that was impossible. I was the bull and Mercedes the worm. I'm sure Mercedes would've liked to be the bull sometimes, not always tagging along in my shadow, waiting for me to say something so that she could simply agree: "Me too."

Never *me*. Always *me too*.

Mercedes never wanted to watch horror movies, but I made her because a girl from school said I wasn't brave enough to watch all the movies she'd seen with her big brother since I didn't *have* a big brother—only Mercedes, the infamous scaredy-cat—and I couldn't stand it, so that afternoon I dragged Mercedes to the video store and we rented all the *Nightmare on Elm Street* movies, and that night and every night after, we had to tell Narcisa to come upstairs to sleep with us because if Freddy gets in your dreams he kills you in your dreams and no one knows what happened to you because it just looks like you had a heart attack or choked to death on your own drool—something "normal"—and so no one ever finds out that you were actually killed by a monster with knives for fingers.

Having siblings can be a blessing. Having siblings can be a curse. We learned this from the movies. And we learned that one sibling always saves the other.

Mercedes started having nightmares. Narcisa and I did everything we could to keep her quiet so Mom and Dad wouldn't find out. They would punish me: horror movies, so obviously the bull's fault. Poor little worm, poor little Mercedes, to have such a beast of a sister, a girl so unlike a girl, so wild, what a cross to bear. Why aren't you more like little Mercedes, so sweet, so quiet, so gentle?

Mercedes's nightmares were worse than any of the movies we watched. They were about school, the nuns, the nuns possessed by the devil—dancing naked, touching themselves down there, appearing in the mirror while she was brushing her teeth or taking a shower. The nuns, like Freddy, taking over her dreams. And we'd never even rented a movie like that.

"What else happened, Mercedes?" I asked, but she didn't say anything, she just screamed.

Mercedes's screams penetrated my skull. They sounded like howls, gashes, bites, animal things. Her eyes were open but she was still somewhere else, and Narcisa and I hugged her so she would come back but sometimes coming back took her a long time, and I thought, once again, that I was stealing something from her, just like when we were in Mom's belly. Mercedes started to get really skinny. We were identical, but less and less so, because I was becoming more and more like a bull and she was becoming more and more like a worm: sunken eyes, hunched, bony.

I never had much love for the Sisters at school nor they for me. In other words, we hated each other. They had a radar for *unruly souls*, that's the term they used, but I didn't mind, I liked the sound of it. I hated their hypocrisy. They were bad people dressed up as good ones. They made me erase all the school's blackboards, clean the chapel, help Mother Superior distribute alms—which was just handing out what other people (our parents) had given to the poor, the middlewoman keeping a bunch for herself, eating expensive fish and sleeping on a feather mattress. It was punishment after punishment for me because I asked why they gave out rice to the poor while they ate sea bass and I told them the Lord wouldn't have liked that because he made the fish for everyone. Mercedes squeezed my arm and cried. She knelt down and prayed for me with her eyes closed tight. She looked like a little angel. While she recited the Hail Mary, I wanted to make everything else stop dead because I felt like my sister's prayer was the only thing worth anything in this fucked-up world. The nuns told my parents that my sister would be perfect for their order, and I imagined her life spent locked away in that prison of horrible clothes and giant crucifixes like shackles: I couldn't bear it.

That summer we got our periods. First Mercedes, then me. Narcisa was the one who taught us how to use pads because Mom wasn't there, and she laughed when we started waddling around like ducks. She also told us that our blood meant that, with the help of a man, we could now make babies. That was ridiculous. Yesterday we couldn't even imagine doing an insane thing like creating a child, and today we could. "That's a lie," we told her. And she grabbed us both by the arms. Narcisa's hands were very strong, big, masculine. Her fingernails, long and pointy, could open sodas without a bottle opener. Narcisa was small and just two years older than us, but she seemed to have lived four hundred more lives. Our arms burned as she repeated that now we had to beware of the living more than the dead—that now we *really* had to be more afraid of the living than of the dead.

"You are women now," she said. "Life isn't a game anymore."

Mercedes started to cry. She didn't want to be a

woman. I didn't either, but I'd rather be a woman than a bull.

One night, Mercedes had another one of her nightmares. There weren't nuns anymore, but men, faceless men who played with her menstrual blood and rubbed it all over their bodies, and then from everywhere monstrous babies appeared, like little rats, to gnaw her to death. I couldn't calm her down. We went to look for Narcisa, but her door was locked from the inside. We heard noises. Then silence. Then noises again. We sat in the kitchen, in the dark, waiting for her. When the door finally opened, we threw ourselves at her, we needed her arms so badly, her hands that always smelled like onion and cilantro, her healing words saying we should be more afraid of the living than the dead. A few inches away, we realized it wasn't her. We stopped, terrified, mute, frozen. It wasn't Narcisa who had come through the door. Our hearts ticked like bombs. There was something both foreign and familiar in that silhouette, filling us with disgust and horror.

I was late to react, I didn't have the chance to cover Mercedes's mouth. She screamed.

Dad slapped each of us across the face and then walked calmly up the stairs.

Neither Narcisa nor her things were in the house the next morning.

GRISELDA

Miss Griselda made amazing cakes.

She had binders filled with photos of the most beautiful cakes in the whole world. It was always the cake, not the new dress. The cake, not the colorfully wrapped gifts. The cake, not the delicious food, that was the highlight of every birthday party: choosing it and imagining all the guests' jealous faces as they saw how awesome our birthday cake was.

The thing was, Miss Griselda's cakes weren't round like everyone else's. They were shaped like Mickey Mouse, a dollhouse, a fire truck, Winnie the Pooh, the Ninja Turtles.

Miss Griselda's cakes weren't white with colored sprinkles like the ones my mom made, or caramel or chocolate like the ones you saw at the other birthday parties. No way. If it was a taxi, the cake was taxicab yellow; if it was a police car, it had everything including the red lights of the siren; if it was a soccer ball, black and white; if it was Cinderella, it had everything down to her blond hair and glass slippers, even the brown mice.

Miss Griselda made unforgettable cakes. She made my brother's First Communion cake in the shape of an open Bible, and on the pages made of sugar she wrote in little gold letters: *There is nothing more perfect than Love. Love always protects, always trusts, always hopes, always perseveres.* People couldn't stop asking my mom where she'd gotten such an amazing cake, and they took pictures of it instead of my brother. Or rather, they took pictures of him, but always with the cake. Mom told Miss Griselda. She blushed, she looked happy.

When it was almost our birthdays, all the kids in the neighborhood would go over to Miss Griselda's after harassing our mothers for days, our stomachs churning with excitement. Finally the moment would come when she would give us her stack of binders and tell us ceremoniously: "Pick whichever one you want. Take your time." Her eyes shone as she waited for us to point to the chosen one.

"This one."

We began to turn the pages. The decision, that terrible moment. And our brothers and sisters always interfering: "Mommy, I want this one for my next birthday," "Mommy, I want her to make me a cake too." We had big fights. Once, we argued so much that Mom got two cakes for my party: one that looked like R2-D2 and another that looked like Strawberry Shortcake.

While we decided, my mom would ask after Miss Griselda's health, about her daughter Griseldita, about her plants. But never about her husband. People said that her husband had gone off with another woman. Or that one day he went to work and never came home.

Or that he was in prison. Or that he beat her so badly she ended up in bed for days and she threatened to call the police. Or that he had kicked her and her daughter out of the house and they'd had to come here. I knew the house well because my friend Wendy Martillo had lived there before her parents got divorced.

Even though it was the same house, Miss Griselda's place was very different from my friend Wendy Martillo's. Maybe it was all the very large and very dark furniture in the tiny living room, or maybe it was the thick curtains that were always shut tight. Miss Griselda's house smelled stale, old, dusty. But none of that mattered, because all you had to do was open one of her binders and it was all bright colors and Disney characters, Barbies, Spider-Man, soccer fields with green-sugar grass, candy goalposts, and cookie-crumb players, hearts, teddy bears, baby booties, treasure chests filled with chocolate coins—anything we could ever wish for on a cake.

Miss Griselda didn't make a living doing this. Actually she didn't charge much at all because everyone in the neighborhood was broke. Her daughter, Griseldita, was the one who supported them. It seemed like she was doing pretty well. She'd gotten two new cars and always wore new clothes. She bought entire suitcases of items from Miss Martha across the street, who brought things from Panama, and it was this woman who spread the rumor that Griseldita was in with a wayward crowd. That's how she said it: "a wayward crowd." Griseldita was blond, very white, and she always wore heels that made her look really tall. She came home at four in the morning a lot, making a ton of noise screeching her brakes, jangling her keys, and click-clacking her heels. What no other woman in the neighborhood would do, Griseldita did.

One day we went to pick out the cake for my eleventh birthday, and as soon as we got inside, my mom, who was in front of me, sent me back outside. But I got a glimpse. Miss Griselda was lying on the floor, her robe askew, her panties showing, and she looked dead. I screamed. My mom was furious, and she sent me home. Then a little later I saw Miss Martha run across the street, then Miss Diana and Miss Alicita. Then the whole block was out on the street. They were shouting for Don Baque, the neighborhood watch, to come help. We peeked out the windows in spite of our mothers' shouted threats.

It seemed that someone had called Griseldita because she arrived shortly, more angry than afraid, and shooed away all the women who had surrounded her mother. She shrieked like a madwoman for all the nosy old ladies to get out, that there was nothing wrong, shitty old ladies, to mind your own business, you bunch of old whores, don't you have your own houses, you bunch of old bats. Miss Martha stood on the sidewalk murmuring, "The nerve of that girl, *her* calling *us* whores. And while we're helping her mother."

My mom was the first to come home because she didn't like all the ruckus. She said just that: "I don't like all the ruckus." She had blood on her hands, and we got scared and started to cry. "Miss Griselda fell down, everything's fine, she's all right, she slipped because she'd just mopped the floor." Later I heard her talking to the other women. Miss Griselda smelled of alcohol, Mom told them, she'd fallen down and busted open her forehead. She was covered in vomit, Mom whispered, and dirty. The other women said that Griseldita might have hit her, that she beats her senseless. They repeated "senseless." My mom didn't believe it. No way, how could a daughter do that to her mother, that's atrocious, no way, no way. The other women said it was true, it was true. And that both of them hit the bottle hard, they hit it hard. They repeated, "They hit the bottle hard, they hit it hard." And that when she came home drunk, she beat her mother. Or when she found her mother drunk, she beat her. That when she was sober, she beat her mother. That it was an everyday thing.

That year on my eleventh birthday, I didn't get my cake. Mom didn't want to order it from Miss Griselda after all that, so we had a sad sponge cake covered in white meringue, Agogó candies for sprinkles, and a candle shaped like the number eleven. Mom promised me that I would have the most spectacular cake in the world for next year, and I started picturing a super tall, super blond Barbie with a crown and a pink princess dress with silver ruffles, all made from layers of cake with caramel in the middle. Miss Griselda would make me the most beautiful Barbie cake in the world. I could already see it, so perfect, in the center of the table. My classmates would die of envy. Bam, bam, bam. One after another, like cockroaches sprayed with Baygon.

That Christmas was brutally hot, and half the neigh-borhood was already out on the street when we heard the gunshot. Boom. Like a thunderclap. Bats took off with terrifying squeals. Dogs started barking. Everyone crowded in front of Miss Griselda's house, but no one dared go inside.

Some police officers brought her out wrapped in a white sheet that was getting soaked with more and more blood, the stain only growing.

"What did Doña Griselda do?" my mom cried. "Or what if it was her daughter?" Miss Martha gasped. And they covered our eyes and sent us home, but none of us went. We just stood a little farther away. The lights from the police car went round and round. Everything was red. In the distance Christmas firecrackers were going off. And the stain kept growing, growing, growing, and a hand escaped from under the sheet. Just one hand, like she was saying, "Ciao, you guys have to stay here."

A few days later a truck came to take away all of Miss Griselda's furniture and a bunch of boxes of her stuff, the cake binders too, I guess. Her daughter left the neighborhood that same day. We never saw her again.

I had shitty round cakes for my birthday the next few years, but honestly, I didn't give a damn about cakes anymore.

NAM

She's getting naked. Something either very bad or very good is happening. Happening to me. Whatever it is, my parents can't find out. I'm at a friend's house. Nothing strange there. But my new friend, half-gringa, half-Ecuadorian, is taking off her uniform, her sports bra, her thong, her shoes. She leaves on her socks, short ones, with a little pink ball at each heel. She's naked, her back to me, staring into her closet.

It's awkward and dazzling. Painful. My head down like an ashamed dog, an ugly, short-legged dog, I try to look the same as I did a moment before, when we were both dressed, when that image, the one of her body, hadn't exploded like a thousand fireworks in my brain. Diana Ward-Espinoza. Sixteen years old. Five-foot-nine. Star player on her high school volleyball team in the United States. Green cat eyes, radioactive. The bright white smile of the people from up there.

Diana, pronounced *Dayana* in gringo, talks and talks, always, nonstop, mixing English and Spanish or making up a third language, hilarious, making me squeal with laughter. With her, I laugh as if there were nothing wrong at home, as if my dad loved me like a dad. I laugh as if I weren't me, but some girl who slept peacefully. I laugh as if cruelty didn't exist.

She repeats the words the teachers say like tongue twisters, and never gets them right. Maybe because of this, because they think she's dumb, or because she lives in a little apartment and not in a majestic house, or because her mom is the English teacher at school and so she doesn't pay tuition, or because she jogs through the neighborhood in tiny shorts, blue with a white line that makes a V on her thighs—because of all that, or because of some obscure hierarchical logic made up by the popular girls, no group has accepted her. She's blond, white, she has green eyes, her tiny nose is dotted with golden freckles, but no group has accepted her.

They haven't accepted me either, but with me it's the same as always: fat, dark, glasses, hairy, ugly, strange.

One day our last names are paired up in computer class. One right next to the other. It's everything. I learn that BFF means Best Friends Forever.

Then we're best friends forever. Then she invites me to her house to study. Then I tell my mom I'm going to spend the night at Diana's. Then we're in her tiny room and she's naked. She turns around to cover her cream-colored body with a denim dress. She turns on music. She dances. Behind her, a gigantic American flag on the wall.

Covered in a fine white fuzz, her skin has the appearance, the delicacy, of a peach. She talks about boys (she likes my brother), about the exam we have the next day (philosophy), about the teacher (he's funny, but what the fuck is *being*?). About how she's never going to understand things like I do, about how I'm the smartest person she's ever met, and about how she, okay, let's be honest, she's good at sports.

She stops in front of the mirror, less than a few feet away from me, on her bed, pretending to be absorbed in our philosophy textbook. If I wanted to, and I do, I could reach out my index finger and touch her hip bone, sliding down to where her pubic hair starts (I've never seen golden pubes), and find out if what glimmers there is wetness.

She ties up her Mary-had-a-little-lamb ringlets, she smears her lips with a gloss that smells like bubble gum, and she complains about her hair, her ears, a pimple I say I can't see. But I can't look at her, and she notices, and she pouts: "You're not even looking at me, stop studying, you already understand what *being* is."

She grabs my chin and raises my face to make me look at her. I smell the bubble gum on her lips. I hear my heart beating. I stop breathing.

"See this pimple? Here? Do you see it?"

My tongue is stuck to the roof of my mouth. I swallow sand. I nod.

We have lunch with her brother Mitch, her twin, who is so handsome that my jaw falls open when I have to talk to him. He was just at soccer practice. He takes off his sweaty shirt and doesn't put on a new one. We eat alone, like a family of three. Diana sets the table, I pour the Coca-Cola, and Mitch mixes sauce into a pot of pasta.

I suppose that their parents, both of them, are

working. I know that Miss Diana, their mom, my English teacher, has another job in the afternoon at a language school. I don't know anything about their dad. I don't ask. I never ask about dads. They tell me that Miss Diana leaves food for them in the morning, that she isn't a good cook. It's horrible. We smother our plates in Kraft parmesan cheese and laugh hysterically.

Mitch has an exam too, but he doesn't want to study. In the dining room, which is also the living room, there are photos on the walls. Mitch and Diana, little, dressed as sunflowers. Miss Diana, thin and young, in front of a house with a mailbox. A black dog, Kiddo, next to a baby, Mitch. The kids at Christmas, surrounded by presents. Miss Diana pregnant. Diana, in white, at her First Communion.

There's something sad in these photos, something in the lighting, typical of gringo photos from the seventies: maybe too many pastel colors, maybe the distance, maybe everything that isn't pictured. I feel a sadness that doesn't belong to me. Mine is still there, but this is a different one. This life—the sunflower children, the beautiful baby beside the black dog, everything that looks so perfect—isn't going to turn out very well. No. Despite their blond heads, their athletic bodies, their pink cheeks, and their bright eyes, it's not going to turn out very well.

There's something desperate, somber, about Diana, about Mitch, about me, about this little apartment where three teenagers are sitting on the floor listening to music.

We play records: the Mamas and the Papas, the

Doors, Fleetwood Mac, Creedence Clearwater Revival, Jimi Hendrix, Bob Dylan, Simon & Garfunkel, the Moody Blues, Van Morrison, Joan Baez.

Diana tells me how her parents went to Woodstock and she pulls out a photo album where, finally, there's a picture of her father. Mr. Mitchell Ward: red mustache, long hair tied with a headband. Ultra gringo, as big and beautiful as his kids, looking at a girl, Miss Diana, almost unrecognizable, so smiling, so natural.

Then, behind that page, there's another photo that makes us all go silent: the dad, dressed as a soldier—Lieutenant Mitchell Ward.

"He went to Vietnam."

The two of them, Diana and Mitch, say the words at the same time, like a single person with a voice that is both masculine and feminine: "He went to Vietnam."

He went to Nam.

Nam.

The shadow reemerges, that suffocating lack of light, silence like an angry sea. The three of us hug our knees and look at the record player. The Doors play, we like them. We sing a little, and Diana translates: *People are strange when you're a stranger / Faces look ugly when you're alone.* Mitch puts on Van Morrison's *Astral Weeks*, and during the song "Madame George," I lie down across Diana's legs. Mitch rests his head on my stomach. We play with one another's hair.

No one studies that evening. We listen to Mr. Mitchell Ward's music, we take turns changing the records and putting them carefully back into their plastic sleeves, into their album covers, and into their spots on the shelf. The movement is slow and sacramental. I imagine that the kids hadn't been able to say goodbye to their father, and that this, lying on the floor and listening to his beloved records, is the prettiest goodbye in the world. And I'm part of it and my heart bursts.

When "Mr. Tambourine Man" comes on, Diana cries. I feel for her hand, and I kiss it with a love so intense that I feel like it's going to kill me. She bends down, she rocks me, she finds my mouth, and just like that, listening to Bob Dylan and through tears, I give, I am given, my first kiss.

Mitch watches us. He sits up, he leans over, he kisses me, and he kisses his sister. The three of us kiss desperately, like orphans, like castaways. Hungry puppies licking up the last drops of milk in the universe. The harmonica plays the melody, *Hey Mr. Tambourine Man, play a song for me.* We sit in the twilight. This is happening. There's nothing more important in the world.

We are the world.

We're almost naked when, from the other side of the door, Miss Diana rummages in her purse looking for her keys, rings the bell, calls to her kids in English.

Diana and I run to her room. Mitch goes into the bathroom. We've grabbed all our clothes, but the record is still playing. Miss Diana wrenches the needle away, and the apartment goes silent. When she opens the bedroom door, Diana and I are pretending to study. Mitch comes out of the bathroom wrapped in a towel, his hair wet. No one admits to having put the record on. Their father's record. The records that belong to Lieutenant Ward, who served in Nam.

Shouting in English. Miss Diana is very red and looks like she's about to cry or burst into a thousand pieces. I hear words I don't understand, and others that I do know the meaning of, words like *fucking* and *fuck* and *records* and *father*. The kids deny everything, and she walks over to Diana. Her hand is open, she's about to hit her, and I, desperate with love, shout for her to stop, that it was me, I put the record on. She doesn't know what to do or say. Her hand is frozen in the air like the Statue of Liberty without a torch, and she remembers that she's my teacher and that I've seen her do something she shouldn't have done, something that stays within the walls of houses, something parents do to their kids when no one is looking.

She leaves without a word.

Diana looks at me. I look at her. I want to hug her, to kiss her, to take her away.

She pulls back her hair and says, "We'd better start studying for philosophy."

We stay up all night studying or pretending to study. She, who doesn't understand any of it, falls asleep in the early morning, and I, in the dim light, study her. She looks like Ophelia, from the painting, and also like She-Ra, He-Man's sister. I pull off the covers to look at her whole body: I wish I were so tiny I could crawl through her half-open lips and live inside her forever. Even the chipped nail polish on her toenails enchants me, it moves me, it excites me. I'd kiss her every pore.

I'm no longer me.

I fall asleep. I dream that Diana is being chased by some black dogs, that she asks me for help and I can't do anything. I hear screams, a man's screams. Even with my eyes open I still hear them. I want to get up, but Diana hugs me tightly and whispers, "It's okay. It's okay."

Daylight arrives with its sounds. Clinking dishes, cleaning up, and, finally, the door slamming behind their mother. Diana gets dressed without showing me her body, but as I'm putting on my uniform, she turns around, lowers the zipper a little, and writes on my back with the tip of her finger, then zips me back up. She smiles. I wear an *I love you* on my back.

I tell Diana that I have to go to the bathroom. She tells me that I'll have to wait to go at school. That's impossible. I got my period in the night, I need to pee, my stomach is upset. I can't wait.

I have to go.

The apartment has two bathrooms. One, for guests, is in the living room, and the other is through the master bedroom, behind the door that's always closed. Mitch is in the front bathroom, and Diana says that he takes a long time, and I'm too embarrassed to ask him to hurry up. I can't do it, much less after yesterday. I can still feel Mitch Ward's lips on my loser neck and my loser belly. I'd rip off my hand before I knocked on that door.

But I can't wait any longer: I'm cold, I'm breaking out in a cold sweat, I have goose bumps. My legs feel weak.

I have to go.

Diana insists that I should go at school, that I can't use her parents' bathroom, even *she* isn't allowed in there, but I know I won't make it, that I'll shit my pants on the way to school, and the uniform is white and I'll die.

It's urgent. I can't wait anymore. I'm not well.

I have to go.

She pulls me out of the house. "Let's go, there are bathrooms at school, we'll be there in just a minute." My forehead is drenched in sweat. It's about to happen, I'm going to shit myself. I tell her that I forgot my book and I go back into the house. I press my legs together, god help me. The only thing I can think about is getting to a bathroom to keep from shitting myself, so that Diana and Mitch won't see me stained with my own excrement. I have to get to a bathroom or I'll die. If I shit myself, I'll never love or be loved again.

I open the door to the master bedroom. It looks like an aquarium filled with thick water, embalming fluid. Lines of dust float in the air, and there's a smell that's stifling, itchy. Sour and sweet and rotten, tear gas, a thousand cigarettes, urine, lemons, bleach, raw meat, milk, hydrogen peroxide, blood. A smell that does not come from an empty room, from a master bedroom.

I'm about to soil my underwear; this is the only thing that gives me courage, the only reason I take another step into the smell that's now like a living creature violently clawing at me. Another step. Another. Now I'm feeling nauseated, now it smells like when there's a dead animal on the side of the road, but I'm already tangled in the guts of that animal, inside it.

I'm dizzy. I grab on to something, and that something is a table, and the table has a lamp on it, which falls and breaks into pieces on the floor. Then, springing up from the bed, with the speed and force of a wave, a lump knocks me to the ground. I can't see. The light is weak, sickly. I don't know what's on top of me. Some shapeless, terrifying thing has fallen on top of me. It's on my chest and I can't move. I try to scream but no sound comes out.

It has a head, it's a monster. Its face, with angry yellow teeth, is stuck to mine. It smells like a carcass. It mutters things I don't understand, makes animal noises, grunts, snorts, it drools on me. It paws and squeezes at my neck, and I see in those red eyes that it's going to kill me, that it hates me and I'm going to die. I'm going to die.

My god.

Please, I say inside my head, please.

Then Diana comes to the door, Diana, She-Ra, He-Man's sister, my savior, comes to the door and shouts something I can't understand, and the beast that's strangling me raises its head toward her and lets go of me.

I start to scream, I vomit, I piss myself and empty my bowels, there, on the carpet.

The light that comes in through the open door allows me to see what was on top of me, killing me. Lying on the floor, it looks like a panting pillow.

"Daddy?"

She approaches him. She doesn't even look at me. She picks him up and I see stumps waving just below his thighs and under his left elbow. Diana tucks him in bed like some atrocious child, who in reality is an emaciated bald man, with bulging eyes and waxy skin. His right arm, the veins on his right arm, are covered in scabs and red wounds. She rocks him and comforts him and kisses his forehead as he cries, and they both repeat over and over, "I'm sorry, I'm so sorry."

I stand up as best I can. Mitch is by the door, glaring at me with hate. I go out into the living room, dial the number to my house. My dad answers. I hang up the phone.

I walk to my grandma's house. There, I lie, I tell her I'm sick, that I couldn't hold it, that I pooped my pants at school. Yes, that's what happened. As I shower, I cry so hard my chest hurts.

Philosophy is the last exam of our last year of high school. My mom writes an excuse for my absence so I can retake the test another day. I get the highest score. I find out that Diana won't be graduating with us, she didn't show up for the exam. They say she's going back to the United States.

I call her. She doesn't answer.

I wait by the telephone. She doesn't call.

Ever again.

I never hear anything else about her. Until recently. I log on to Facebook and find a message from a former high school classmate:

"Hello, I'm sorry to give you this news, but did you know that Diana Ward was killed in an attack in Afghanistan? She and her wife were in the US Army. I wanted to let you know because I remember that you were good friends. Isn't it sad?"

PUPS

Vanesa and Violeta, the twins, next-door neighbors my whole life, now live abroad. They left some fifteen years ago, like me, and haven't set foot back in the country since. They brought their mom over, then their older brother, their sister-in-law, and their nieces and nephews, and the only one who stayed behind in the old house in the neighborhood was the middle brother, the weird one.

Everyone knows you can't go home again. After the hugs and the tears comes the real reunion: you're left face-to-face with the same people even though you're different now, standing in front of people you don't recognize. No one in front of no one. The charade of how nice it all is, how delicious, how much it was all missed. They look for you in the same places but you're not there, you look for them in the same places but they're not there—and that's where the tragedy begins.

After a few days at home, going through the motions, feigning tranquility like a circus lion, letting yourself be bathed in the sticky familial gaze, the time comes when you can't take it anymore: acting like you've come home requires an exhausting effort. It could kill you.

I go next door to visit the neighbor, the weird one, because, I tell myself as I walk the ten steps that separate our houses, I want to hear about his sisters, but in reality I want to know about *him*: the one left behind in the family exodus. Him: the boy from my childhood.

He opens the door in his robe, a flannel robe, and in these parts it's always sweltering, but the robe is flannel, plaid, above the knee. He wears blue flip-flops like he's going to the pool. He does not wear pants, but he does wear glasses, which he straightens with a little tap to the bridge of his nose when he sees me standing on the other side of the metal door painted white. He's so pale that he looks like he's from a sunless world, the canary in the coal mine, but it's just that he never leaves the house. He has lost all his hair, gained about fifty pounds; he smells like an abandoned elderly person. Of course he recognizes me, of course he says my name, of course he invites me in to sit on the same red sofa that's now faded and covered in hair, as if cats lived there, but there are no cats. He knows who I am. But more importantly— I know who he is. Face-to-face, there's no lapse in time. I never left, he never stayed behind.

After three idiotic questions that he answers looking away with his same old stutter—How are your sisters and brother? Your mom? Why didn't they ever come back?—I kneel on the red rug, a fake Persian, filthy, and I open his robe, underneath which he wears nothing, and I begin to suck his cock. He isn't startled. I am, because the smell is repulsive and his pubes are shaved and his cock is dead, but I keep going and going and going until he gets hard, and I keep going longer still until he comes in my mouth and I swallow it and it tastes like Dijon mustard and bleach. Beside my knee an enormous cockroach crawls by and he smashes it into the fake Persian rug. Then I realize that all over the rug there are a bunch of dead cockroaches, bellies up, stiff legged, and that, in fact, I'm kneeling on one that died a while ago, that's now just a fossil of a cockroach, a shell. From the pocket of his robe he takes out a filthy handkerchief and wipes the corners of my lips. We don't speak.

While he's in the kitchen I look around the living and dining rooms. You can hardly call this place a house, it's so filled with stuff: black garbage bags, empty bottles, cardboard boxes, stuffed animals. Cockroaches climb up and down the walls and one marches boldly up to my foot. I'm terrified of them, but I can't move, suddenly I'm so exhausted, a sailor stepping onto dry land after a long journey, that I'd lie down on this rug covered in hair, dead skin, bug corpses, and dust without thinking twice.

He brings me a foul-smelling glass of flat Coca-Cola that's covered in greasy fingerprints. He waits for me to drink it all, and then takes my hand to help me stand.

"Want to see them?"

I met Vanesa and Violeta, who were identical, at the park on the corner. When they told me they were my same age, had two brothers, and lived in the red house next door to mine, I thought it was incredible. Their family was just like mine, everything the same, except there were two of them instead of one. I was just me, and that was boring. I was fascinated by the twin thing: I asked them questions nonstop, and the two of them, with their identical faces, like a girl talking to herself in the mirror, responded in unison. One day they told me that if one of them was in pain, the other one was too, so I pinched Vanesa, and Violeta screamed. I applauded like I'd seen real magic, and decided that I loved them: my magical friends, like loving a circus act. That trick, of hurting one of them so that the other felt it, was one I repeated many times. I punched them in the stomach, pulled their hair, stepped on their fingers, poured hot wax on their legs, stuck tacks under their fingernails. They always felt it at the same time, and they cried, but they let me do it: They were the most innocent girls in the world. The most.

My twelfth birthday came a month after meeting them, and I invited them without asking permission. They showed up wearing identical plaid dresses with lace collars, each with one hand on a huge gift-wrapped package. My mom adored them for being so elegant, for still being such little girls, for being so polite, and for giving me a doll with enormous eyelashes on her blue eyes that opened and closed. I was always terrified of that doll, and my mom tried everything, even baptized her with holy water, but finally she had to hide her, because in my nightmares, Dina, which was the doll's name according to the box, would strangle me with her little hands, which had suddenly grown into huge red claws. My brothers called her Devilina, and sometimes, at night, they'd bring her into my room and leave her on my bed, seated, looking at me with those fixed, stunned eyes. They made her talk, saying horrible things: that she was going to take me to hell with her because I was as bad as she was. My brothers tortured me with Devilina for months and months until my dad punched them each in the back, and if they hadn't shielded themselves first, he would've punched them in the head too.

"Stop messing with your sister or you'll make her even crazier."

Vanesa and Violeta had those dolls all over their room, it was horrifying. I could never be alone in there. When they left because they had to go to the bathroom or were thirsty, I would wait in the hallway. On one of those afternoons, a door opened and I met their middle brother, the weird one, for the first time. He asked me if I wanted to see something and I said yes, because all my life I've wanted to see things and because I've always said yes to men. He took me out onto the balcony, and there, in a cage, were two hamsters twitching their little noses and their little mouths, staring off into space like idiots. He told me that the female had just had pups and that she had eaten them. I didn't believe him until he stuck his hand in the cage and pulled out half of a little hamster, a tiny pink thing, with just one paw and a nose with a little blood still on it, and a head the size of the spitballs the girls at school hit me in the neck with. The mother hamster, furry and chubby cheeked, stared ahead with her little black eyes and her cartoonlike whiskers. It was hard to imagine her eating her pups, but then there the middle brother was, with his palms open, showing me pieces of baby hamster, the paw and nose in his right hand, the little head in his left, and telling me that he'd seen the whole thing, from the birth to the act of cannibalism. Then he told me that the mother hamster was very smart not wanting her babies to grow up in that house, his house, and he threw the pieces of flesh off the balcony, wiped his hands on a handkerchief that he took out of his pocket, unzipped his pants, pushed my head down, and told me to kneel, open my mouth, and put it around that other piece of pink flesh that he had between his legs. He ordered me not to use my teeth, and I did what he said. All this happened in front of the hamsters, and who knows how many of our neighbors. This was love, he explained to me, and I said yes because I've always said yes to men.

I was twelve and he was thirteen. What did either of us know about love.

I waited for Vanesa and Violeta in the hall. I told them about the mother hamster, and they said, without surprise or disgust, that it wasn't the first time, that she always ate her pups, but that their parents had explained that it was okay because the newborn hamsters were too weak, that they wouldn't have survived, and that rodents ate their young when they knew that the world would eat them up anyway. They accepted it so naturally that I almost told them that their brother had put his little piece of meat in my mouth because that was love. But I didn't. I went home and had mashed potatoes and chicken nuggets for dinner. My dad, like always, had my mom bring dinner up to him in his room. He sometimes tried to have dinner with us, but the dining room became the twilight zone: us gobbling our food in silence like deranged creatures, Mom burning the rice, spilling the soup, laughing at nothing, like our house was a loony bin and not a house. That night I told them about the hamsters but not about the other thing, and one of my brothers said, "That's disgusting," and the other said, "Don't talk about shit like that while we're eating," and punched me in the arm. My mom was in the kitchen. She offered more chicken nuggets and mashed potatoes and they said yes and I did too, but I was swallowing my tears because at my house when you're drowning, you eat, and when no one saves you, you eat, and when you're purple, bloated, and dead, you eat. Mom wouldn't have done anything anyway.

From my room I could hear Vanesa and Violeta. Sometimes they'd shout my name and I'd tell my mom I was going next door. Never the other way around: my dad didn't like people over at the house. Vanesa and Violeta's dad was named Tomás—Don Tomás, we called him—and he was scary. He was a very tall, very pink man who had glasses with thick black frames, wore white suits, and was almost never home. When he was, we had to lower our voices to whispers, and the air was filled with an electric energy, wet, like when a huge storm is coming, and then our games would take a dark turn. We'd kill the dolls in horrible ways, we'd play dead ourselves, or we'd throw the toys violently, cruelly, into the toy box. In the quiet you could hear the squeal of the hamster wheel as the creatures tried desperately to escape into oblivion.

Those days I'd slowly stand up, float down the stairs like a ghost, open the door gasping for breath, and go back to my house, where the air was no better, but at least it was mine. You can always breathe your own air, even if it's terrible, because it's what your lungs yearn for without knowing why. The sad intelligence of the lungs. Flesh of my flesh. Air of my air. Daughter of my parents.

Vanesa and Violeta's mother was short, and that's all she was. As much as I think about her, I can't remember any other distinctive trait. She was like a stain walking around in a dress. Her name was maybe Margarita, maybe Rosa, something cutesy like that, floral.

After the encounter on the balcony, I didn't see the weird middle brother for a while. I knew he knew when I came over because his door would open a crack and I could feel his black eyes following me as I walked down the hall. Sometimes, when I walked by his room, I'd feel an animal heat in my groin that made me dizzy, but it was nothing like when I was sick. If I heard that the hamster had once again given birth and eaten her pups, I'd get all excited. Since the rodent's cannibalism always happened at night, I suggested the twins take photos, but I wasn't going to use my dad's camera and they weren't going to use their father's—they'd burn our hands—so I had to go without seeing it.

After about a year I started to get bored with Vanesa and Violeta. I called them Vaneta or Vionesa, but they didn't get mad; they never showed any emotion besides high-pitched laughter or stoic tears. I was no longer amused by the trick of hitting one and hurting the other, but I kept doing it anyway. Now I only went to their house in order to walk down the hall where I knew he was, shut inside with his weird things—books, bugs, fishbowls, comics—and I'd sit on the floor and play with his sisters just to feel close to him, to hear his cough. In the mornings, when we left for school at the same time, we didn't look at each other, but I could feel my face burning and my heart pounding. I thought that everyone could tell, but the truth is that no one was looking at me. Ever. My brothers looked at me at night when they wanted to scare me with the evil doll, but that was it. One day I went over to their house, like always, and he came out of nowhere, grabbed my hand, and pulled me into his room, quickly, without saying a word. There, in the dimness that reeked of used socks and unwashed armpits, he looked at me, he straightened his glasses on the bridge of his nose, and he kissed me, he kissed me a lot, he kissed me standing and lying down, and I let him kiss me, standing and lying down. This time he didn't have to say that this was love because I already knew it.

I knew it perfectly.

When their father left them, my dad didn't want me to go over there anymore because it was a house without a head. That's how he said it, or maybe he said something else, like without a head of the family, but I only remember him saying "house without a head," like a decapitated chicken, crazed. It wasn't difficult for me, because I didn't want the twins in my life anymore. I'd discovered books and with them the delicious feeling of not needing anything or anyone else in the world. I wasn't a weird little girl anymore, but a book-ish little girl. Sometimes I imagined the twins on the other side of my wall, of my mirror, surrounded by their terrifying porcelain dolls, playing patty-cake like little retards. Nature had duplicated its mistake. I didn't feel sorry for them at all.

Him, the weird brother, I saw when we all left for school, and my mom, in a hurry, like she was nervous, would say hello to Margarita or Rosa, their mother, and tell her that someday she'd stop by for a cup of cof-fee. Meaning never, of course. One day, I must've been fifteen by then, I stopped seeing him in the morning. He graduated, and no one ever asked about his exis-tence. I was dying to know, but I pictured myself melt-ing onto the asphalt as I uttered his name, pronouncing the last syllable from a puddle of myself. My brothers had graduated too, all the young people had become people: the damage was already done.

I graduated too, started university, finished, con-tinued saying yes to men, breaking like a cheap glass against the walls of different houses. Or rather, grow-ing. Shortly after I left the country, my dad, that man who I wanted so badly to love me—the worst form of love—died before I ever really knew him, and I ran in a thousand circles like the hamsters on their idiotic wheel, and finally I returned and I walked the ten steps to his, the middle brother's, house.

"You want to see them?"

I say yes because I've always said yes to men. I stand and follow him up the stairs I haven't climbed in years, in a thousand lifetimes, maybe ever. The stench, like the place has been abandoned, has taken over the upper level as well, and there's a new obstacle at every step. I don't know what all that shit is, but I know if I fall I will never be able to get up, that I will sink into the soft accumulation of trash and remain there forever, like a bug trapped in amber, like Alice falling and falling down the rabbit hole. Wonderland: a third world house choked with garbage. The white rabbit: the weird brother who was abandoned by everyone. He puts his hand on my hand and leads me to his room, the one that was always his.

There, as if no time has passed, a pair of hamsters run around a wheel. He turns on the light, a disgusting light, a naked bulb, and I see that there are photos on all the walls, photos enlarged to the point of disfigurement: enormous hamsters, step by step, determinedly, devouring their pups. Adorable little rodent teeth sunk into the pinkish flesh of tiny alien-faced things, their own young. The photos I always wanted to see are right in front of my eyes, and they are more beautiful than I ever imagined. Creatures eating the creatures they gave birth to. Mother feeding on her offspring. Nature correcting its mistakes. We look at each other. I smile. He smiles.

I understand when I feel that tickling in my groin, that dizziness, that hand sliding under my skirt electrocuting me, that sometimes, only sometimes, you can go home after all.

BLINDS

What you have to do is close the windows and lower the blinds in the daytime, then open everything up at night. That's what we've done day after day, summer after summer, for as long as this house, which my great-grandparents built, has had windows.

The person in the family in charge of raising and lowering the blinds—responsible for the temperature inside the house, you could say—has always been a child on their way out of being a child. Who was the first? Some uncle or aunt, who we only heard about in reference to one of my or my cousins' physical traits. Relatives who one day went off to war or to the United States, emigrated and never returned, or who died in childhood and left behind Julio's nose, María Teresa's bowlegs, my stutter. Or nothing—relatives who passed through this family like the maids walked through this house when my grandfather was still alive: silent, hunched, never interrupting. Those only mentioned to recall how many children my great-grandmother, Aunt Elsa, Great-Aunt Toya, and Grandma had had, and how many had died. Back then, I suppose, kids just died like three of Laika's seven puppies, which were thrown in the trash.

"Mom, if I died, what would you do?"

"I'd die too, Felipe, I'd die too. You are the only man in my life, the only one who will never leave me."

Two summers ago, the person in charge of the house's temperature was my cousin Julio, who was fourteen, but Mom says that my aunt and uncle bought an apartment at the beach and that's why they stopped coming. Every time we see each other in the city, less and less now, they promise us that they'll come this summer, for sure. But two hundred thousand days of summer in this town have passed, and they've never come.

This house was a different house when my aunt and uncle used to come with Julio and María Teresa: they filled it up and kept the pool clean and brought Laika, we played in town without anyone watching us, we stayed up late, slept on blankets on the patio under the stars, which we don't have in the city, and talked about things we don't talk about in the city.

Nothing that is here is there.

Not even us.

In this house, our house, it was like we were different from the people we were in our apartments. There, we were smaller, clumsier, uglier, stinkier. That is to say, there, in the city, we were losers. At school I didn't have a single friend, but during the summer I was part of a group. A group of just three, true, but there was a girl. The funniest girl in the world, my cousin María Teresa, and the coolest guy in the world, my cousin Julio. And, well, me.

In this house, in the armpit of that town, in the armpit of the world, life was pretty good. The three of us grew up here. Here, Julio broke my arm while pretending to be Bruce Lee. Here, we cut the hair off of María Teresa's dolls, and she didn't talk to us for the rest of the summer. Here, we found out that Dad wouldn't be coming back from his vacation abroad, that his vacation abroad was named Sofía, and that Sofía was going to have a baby, my future brother or sister. Here, María Teresa got her first period and my uncle cried and my aunt called him a fag. Here, we drank and we smoked. Here, Julio told me for the first time about jacking off and showed me a porn magazine, and I stared at all the pussies in it till I had them memorized. Here, María Teresa's body changed, she stretched out—but we never stopped calling her María Obesa—and she became a woman with everything women have, plus the black hair and cheek dimples that had been María Teresa's her whole life. Here, Julio became a hateful, acne-ridden creature who never stopped popping his zits and telling everyone to fuck off. Here, I was scared to death when I saw Julio's huge body and closed fist coming at my face because I called him a fag. Here, my cousin Julio broke my nose.

Here, one stormy summer night, in the pool, María Teresa kissed me on the mouth and then told Julio, and at first he called us pigs, disgusting, but then he also wanted to. The three of us kissed, María Teresa in the middle, kissing me and kissing him. It felt so wildly good and so wildly bad all at once, and it jumbled up our hearts so much that we all ended up crying. Julio cried. María Teresa cried. I cried. It felt like we'd spent our whole lives in that pool, alone, without any adult ever holding up a towel and telling us to get out. We kissed each other's wet, wrinkled mouths again, and we swore that we'd love each other forever, that when we grew up, we'd get married. The three of us. That there would never be anyone but us. That we'd be better parents to our children, that we'd never leave them like my dad did, that we'd never put work above everything like my uncle did, that we'd never be as stupid as my aunt, that we'd never be as sad as my mom.

On the wall of the toolshed, the headquarters of our club, we drew a heart with our initials inside. And another and another, until there were many hearts and many initials on the old walls of the shed. Then we cut our thumbs with my uncle's knife and joined them together.

Then we kissed.

It was obvious: we'd be better parents than our parents because we actually loved one another.

Here, one of my uncle's employees, who had come out into the yard to tell us that we were going to catch a cold, saw us kissing and touching each other.

But now they don't come here anymore. The pool is full of leaves and little insect corpses, which surround me as I float, still, absorbed. Sometimes I think that the sun doesn't even touch me, that this fucking town's violent sun, which makes everyone else so tan and happy, avoids me entirely. I feel just as pale and out of place as I do in the city.

I hit a ball against the wall, again and again, possessed,

and imagine the growl of my uncle's truck engine, Laika's barks, María Teresa's high-pitched laugh, Julio juggling a soccer ball, my mom telling her brother how happy she is to see him, and seeing her happy, really happy, after so many months of living with something else, something else that is not happiness. To hear her sing love songs, to watch her go into the kitchen to make lemonade, serve ice cream in those tall glasses that can fit two scoops, whipped cream, and a wafer. Your uncle first, your uncle, your uncle, your uncle. You, go away, don't touch it, slapping my hand away.

None of that happens anymore. I don't know the names of the dogs barking in the distance, and the tall glasses collect dust on the shelf. I stay in the pool, a translucent bug floating among the other dark bugs. Mosquitoes buzz by my eyelashes. I don't move. I hardly breathe. I have gone so long without moving that I think the best thing that could happen to me now would be to die, to drown, so that María Teresa and Julio, full of sunshine and shellfish and friends and whatever else they have there at that fucking beach, will have to scream and sob over me. Me, their love, their husband, who they left abandoned in this cursed house in the country with two crazy, lonely, evil women for the only happy months of the fucking year. That's just not right, for fuck's sake. They will sob and sob until the last summer of their lives when, old and stooped, punished by heartbreak and loneliness and hideousness and poverty and dementia, their senile minds will still remember their beloved Felipe, who drowned because of them, because they did nothing, because they didn't say: Mom and Dad, we want to go to the country to be with Felipe, there's nothing better than that, we choose Felipe over everything else.

Fucking idiots.

But I don't drown in the end.

Mom calls me to dinner.

I didn't feel like lowering the blinds today and the heat is unbearable. The only one who can say anything about it is Mom, because Grandma, although she surely notices, can't complain: for the past few years, her face has been frozen in the same look of surprise, one shoulder slumped, one hand, the right one, folded over her thigh, and the other covering it up in shame, as if it were her pussy. Sitting there, in her wheelchair, Grandma looks so small, so harmless. But she used to be a mean old bitch who would smack you so hard with that same hand, the right one, so hard that your face would be red for hours. Julio once told us that she called him a son of a bitch, said, "I know you're not my son's child," as she beat him. She once called María Teresa a slut just for wearing a miniskirt—"Little slut, little slut, little slut, worthless sluts, you and your mother both." To me, on the other hand, and I don't know if it was because she liked me or pitied me, she just said, "Sad. You're a sad boy."

After the blood clot, she stopped talking, thank god. At first she would write down what she wanted on pieces of paper, but the notes were so insulting that Mom had to read her messages omitting every other word. The old lady wanted to retain her freedom of expression so badly that her knuckles would go white against the arms of her wheelchair and she looked like she was about to scream, her eyes about to pop out of their sockets, like her rage could trigger an earthquake. Then she'd soil herself. Mom took the notebook away from her. She left her mute.

At dinner, Mom says that she's not going to eat, that she's going to take a shower, that the heat is too unbearable. She also says that there's tuna salad and bread in the refrigerator. I eat guiltily: the heat is my fault, her lack of appetite is my fault, and eating this bad dinner alone is my punishment. Because of the blinds. But I don't want to be the one in charge of the blinds; the ones who raise and lower the blinds in this house always leave, die, are forgotten. No. I don't want to. I miss my cousins—I want to be the boy I was when they were here.

I begin to cry.

This summer, and very possibly every summer for the rest of my life, is going to be shit.

I start to feel scared of the house. I think of all the men who are no longer here: Grandpa, Dad, Uncle, Julio. I don't want to be here either. I don't like being a man. Can't I be something else? There's no other place I want to go, unless the past is a place, but I don't want to be here.

I go upstairs with a bowl of salad for Mom. She's lying under the fan, faceup, still soaking wet from the shower, still naked. Mom's body, white as cream, like mine, lit by the dim light coming in from the window, looks like the body of a drowned woman, like someone who's been pulled from a pool, too late, and laid out, legs splayed, on the bed.

With Mom dead, I could go. Yes. I'd throw some

things in a backpack and I'd go off to find María Teresa and Julio. Mom dead. Drowned. I didn't lower the blinds.

"Mom?"

I start crying again. I lie down next to her.

She opens her eyes, tells me everything is fine.

"My baby boy, my baby boy, my sweet boy, come here, give me a kiss."

I move closer and she caresses my face, tells me I look like Dad. Like that summer with María Teresa and Julio, our lips touch.

"You came from here," she says, and puts my hand on her damp pussy.

"And you drank from here," she says, and moves my hands to her sagging breasts.

I squeeze them and I kiss them and I suck them, thinking the whole time about my cousins, and the love we said we'd always have for each other.

I hear her voice, a voice that comes from deep underwater.

"Do you want to marry me, son?"

I say yes. Everyone's abandoned me, so I say yes.

When I turn toward the door I think I see Grandma there, in her wheelchair, a repulsive smile on her face.

Mom whispers, "You came from here, my son, enter, here, come."

CHRIST

It all began when my baby brother's fever started getting worse.

I'd missed school for so many days it felt like I'd never even gone, that since I was born the only thing I'd ever done was take care of my baby brother. I stayed home while Mom went to work, and I gave him a spoonful of the pink medicine every hour and the clear medicine every four.

She had given me a clock with big numbers for my birthday.

The baby was light, he barely weighed a thing. It was like carrying wrinkled tissue paper in my arms. He didn't giggle. He rarely opened his eyes.

One night, one of my mom's friends punched a hole through the bathroom door, sick of hearing him cry.

"Shut it up," he said to my mom. "Make that fucking creature shut up. If you weren't such a whore, you wouldn't have made such a monster. You should put it out of its misery."

He cursed repeatedly and continued punching the door with his fist.

It was better he hit the bathroom door and not my baby brother. And not her. But he hit her some too.

We never saw that friend again, and it got harder to buy the pink medicine and the clear medicine, but she made it stretch with a little bit of boiled water.

She clenched her fists while waiting to take my baby brother's temperature. Her fingers would be white after. And she made a little noise after shaking the thermometer in the air and looking at it under the lamp. A little noise with her tongue and teeth. When she didn't make the noise it meant the baby was having a better day.

Some weekends she sent me to my grandparents' house.

My grandpa Fernando would always take me to the cemetery to visit his dead mother, Rosita, first. Then we would go to La Palma to drink Coca-Cola with vanilla ice cream. A little girl with her grandpa. In a dress. With no brothers or sisters. An only child. Spoiled. It always flew by, and it was Monday before I knew it.

One afternoon while I was watching *Woody Woodpecker*, my baby brother started to cry. I didn't go to him. It was time for the pink medicine, but I didn't go. I wanted to watch *Woody Woodpecker*. The whole episode. For once in my life, a whole episode without having to look at the clock with the big numbers, without having to measure out the medicine with that big white plastic spoon, without having to fight to get him to swallow it, my clothes all sticky and smelly with the stuff, like always. I wanted to smell like a girl who watched *Woody Woodpecker* and did nothing else. I laughed, even at the parts that weren't funny.

Loud, very loud, like Woody, to block out my brother's cries.

After a while, the show ended and *The Flintstones* started. I watched that whole episode too.

When I went to check on him, the baby had stopped shrieking. I touched him. It was like putting my hand over a bright candle.

I called the neighbor, and the neighbor called my mom.

"Did you give him the pink medicine?"

I nodded.

The doctor sent us some green medicine and suppositories.

My mom showed me how to give him the suppositories. I didn't want to. My baby brother screamed like this little brown dog that was hit by a taxi once in front of our house and then left to die, with his guts on the pavement, but still alive. He screamed exactly like that.

Pink, clear, green, suppository.

The next day, we left my brother with my grandparents and went to Cristo del Consuelo Church. It was in the black neighborhood, the forbidden neighborhood. My mom and I were like two scoops of vanilla ice cream floating in Coca-Cola.

A large black woman told my mom to have faith.

"Have faith, Doñita. Christ works miracles."

Then she asked for money, spare change. Why didn't she ask her Christ? If he could work miracles, he must be rolling in spare change, not like us, who sometimes had to walk places because we didn't have enough to cover the bus fare.

The black lady sold my mom a little baby doll to hang from Christ's brown robe. When we got inside the church, there were tons of those little dolls everywhere. And little hearts and little legs and little arms and little heads and other body parts I didn't recognize. And photos and cards and bills and drawings. One of the cards read, *Help lord Im only nine years od and I hav cancer.*

"Mom?" I asked. "How is Christ going to know which of all these babies is my baby brother?"

"Because He is very smart."

It smelled strange in there. Like old people, dust, like when I don't wash my hair for days, like heat, like when the power goes out.

Before we left, my mom took out an empty bottle of Los Andes ketchup and filled it with water from a faucet.

"Good water," she said. "Water from this sweet Christ, holy water."

She gave me a sip, but it didn't taste holy; it tasted like ketchup and a little rusty, and I thought to myself that water with ketchup—like what we put on our rice at the end of the month, when the bottle was running out—could not possibly work miracles. Holy water should taste like caramel, like a double hamburger. It shouldn't taste like poor people. With that stupid taste in my mouth, I wanted to scream at the whole world that they were wrong, that the only miracle here was this woman getting change for selling little body parts and whole little bodies to stick on the skirt of a Christ who tasted like watery ketchup. My little brother stayed there, or rather, a little doll just as deformed as he was, surrounded by hundreds of other equally creepy little dolls and heads and arms and legs and hearts, like there had been some kind of explosion.

"He has to stay there," my mom said, suddenly furious.

And I cried the whole way home because I realized that she didn't know what she was doing either.

At home, my mom gave my baby brother a little bit of that water and poured some on his head. He opened his eyes and showed us his mouth, toothless. Finally, he smiled at us.

The following week, just like that, with that same smile, we put him inside a tiny white box that the neighborhood took up a collection to pay for.

I'm back at school now. Back in fourth grade again, where I'm huge and I don't have any friends.

When they ask me if I have brothers or sisters, I think about that little baby hanging from the Cristo del Consuelo's robes, and I say no.

They wouldn't understand.

PASSION

Curled into a ball on the ground, you look like a bundle some beggar left there without fearing that anyone might steal it because there is nothing of value in a bag so filthy. It's you. The dust kicked up by the crowd's sandals—the crowd rushing to see the spectacle—covers you completely. You have a mouth full of sand, and a pointy stone juts into your sternum. Someone steps on you. You remain still. A hungry wild dog sniffs you. You remain still. You think of poison, of bitter, murderous roots, of the sharp fangs of the desert snakes that you've milked so many times, you think about ending everything swiftly.

You know, the only thing you know, is that you're not going to be able to live without him. What you *don't* know, and what you will never know, is that he loved you. That is something that can only be known by someone who has been loved before. You are not one of those people. Your mother left you, snotty and skinny and naked. A little wet creature on your grandparents' doorstep.

She went looking for men, the people in town said

in hushed tones. They used a word to speak of her that later—not much later—also became yours, that fit you like a tailored suit, that was transmitted to you like a virus.

You don't know, either, that your mother wanted to save you from herself, from the thing that you inherited from her and that seems as much a blessing as a curse.

The first prophecy you fulfilled was *you are just like your mother.* They hit you so that you wouldn't be just like your mother as they screamed that you were just like your mother. One night, you must've been twelve, thirteen, you were late getting home from your favorite pastime: picking roots, herbs, and flowers to later boil them, smash them up, mix them together to see what would happen. You ran back with your bag full, kicking up dust with your sandals, dirtying the bottom of your skirts, and the people who saw you running by, sweaty, panting, shook their heads as if they were saying, *poor thing*, as if they were saying, *she's just like her mother.*

She, your grandmother, and he, your grandfather, beat you so hard that you lost your hearing in your right ear and to this day walk with a limp. With a switch made of laurel—that switch made of laurel—they ripped up your back, your buttocks, your tiny chest, until shreds of flesh hung loose, like a half-peeled orange.

They shouted and shouted, they whipped you and whipped you. Their shadows in the firelight looked like furious giants. You closed your eyes. You curled into a ball on the floor, gripped the gray stone your mother had left tied around your neck, and said to yourself, *If they don't kill me, I'll show them.*

They didn't kill you.

You woke before dawn choking on your own blood. You spit, vomited, and with an agonizing pain, managed to sit up. Slowly, very slowly, you covered each of your wounds with poultices and wrapped them in rags. You went to your bag, you found a bowl, and there, in darkness, you mixed several herbs and roots in the mortar with some drops of a liquid that glowed yellow in the moonlight.

No one saw this.

You put the bowl with the mixture on the fire, whispered some words—they sounded like a chant, a prayer, a spell—covered the gray stone with your palm, picked up your things, and left.

When they found your grandparents, they were dry, dehydrated, stiff like those dead snakes that sometimes appear on the roads.

The ones who found them said that they were purple, that their eyes were bulging and their jaws were open inhumanly wide.

The ones who found them said that they looked like they'd died of terror.

They lost track of you for many years. Another lost girl in a world of lost girls. Some said you had joined up with the nomads and traveled from town to town, dancing and showing your breasts for coins. Others swore you had killed some men who had tried to take the necklace—the stone—your mother had given you. Others were convinced that you had died a leper, fallen to pieces and alone. That someone knew someone who knew someone who had seen you agonizing in a leper colony, locked in a dungeon with other murderers, dancing naked for horny men.

In reality, your life didn't matter to anyone, and the only thing they wanted to know was what the hell you had done to your grandparents to dry them out like dead branches.

They started to call you other things too, just like your mother, and they used you, used your name, to scare their children.

One day you heard that there, in that cursed land you swore you'd never set foot in again, was a special man that you had to meet. You will never be able to clearly understand why, but you undid everything you'd built over many years. You walked miles and miles, wearing your sandals to shreds, and you arrived at dawn, barefoot, your hair matted, your skin burnt.

He seemed to be waiting for you. He asked for a bowl of clean water, and he bent down to wash, with an almost feminine delicacy, your scabbed and dirty feet. You will never be able to clearly understand why, maybe because this was the only act of kindness anyone had ever shown you—creature of beatings, daughter of brutality, princess of the nights that end with wounded women—but in that moment, you made the decision to give your life to him, to do whatever he might want, anything, to be clay in his hands, his, his servant.

He asked you your name, and he repeated it with a sweetness that made you cry your first tears, your tears, girl, that would become legendary. Then he held out his hand and he dried your tears and he said—yes, you weren't imagining things, he said it—that he loved you.

He said, "I love you."

There was no turning back. You who were humiliated, orphaned, mistreated, crippled, half-deaf—the whore, the murderer, the leper—no longer existed, and would never exist again.

Standing before him, you were you.

And standing before him, you were an extraordinary woman. The best of all women.

And if a dog, which is a being of limited understanding, faithfully follows the one who pets his head and back, how could you not follow him down into hell itself? How could you not do even the impossible to make him happy, to help him keep his promises? So, like a grateful dog, you sat at his feet to watch him, to listen to him, entranced, crazed with love, as if from his mouth flowed honey, grapes, jasmine, birds.

Sometimes, as he told his sweet stories of fishermen and shepherds, you would grip your gray stone, and twenty, thirty, forty people would appear to listen to him like you did: with a childlike devotion, as if he were a magus, as if from his mouth flowed honey, birds.

You knew that made him happy.

Suddenly he had many followers. He changed. His stories became recipes; his anecdotes, orders. He started to talk about things that you didn't understand, that no one really understood, things that were magical, sacred, maybe even sacrilegious. None of that mattered to you.

The others no longer let you touch him—except for his tunic, his sandals—and he no longer visited your tent with such frequency, with such urgency. You held on to the memory of the desert man's scent that didn't fade from your nose, your body, your dress. A smell that never faded, that made you tremble until the last second of your life. He was yours, sent from heaven, he now said, but yours. And you were his. That's why you gripped the stone around your neck when they ran out of wine at that wedding, and why you made fish and bread appear where there had been nothing but rocks and sand—because in your loneliness you learned that water, rocks, sand would obey you.

That's also why you applied, without anyone seeing you, without anyone wanting to see you, your unguent to the white eyes of the beggar, who opened them and said *miracle*, and then you hid in the man's tomb to fill his dead lungs with the essence of life—invoking forces you shouldn't have, death is death, but it had become far too late to turn back—and you made the corpse rise up, walk, and the man was crowned—more and more each day—with glory.

But you wouldn't allow it to happen. Allow him to die. No: allow him to let himself be killed. You weren't going to allow that. You tried to stop him, you told him about the unguent, about the rocks that were food, the wine that was water, about the white, useless eyes of that beggar, about the corpse that walked, about the stone you wore around your neck, about the forces you invoked, infinitely more powerful than you and he. But he didn't believe you. He pushed you away from him violently—him, violently—and you fell, and from the ground you looked up at him and you saw god. That man was your god. And you called yourself a liar, you called yourself a trickster, you called yourself crazy, and he said to you:

"Get out of my sight, woman."

If a dog will guard the doorway of the man who gives it a crust of bread, if a dog will bare its fangs and rip anyone to shreds in order to protect that man, how could you not defend him even from himself, from his own convictions? That's why the day they took him and subjected him to all those horrible things, you gripped the stone and the sky clouded over until it became a mass of gray lava, and your sobs—oh, your sobs—made people thousands of miles away cry into their soup, cry as they made love, as they tilled the earth, as they washed their clothes in the river, as they dreamed.

When his head lies on his chest, inert, you curl into a ball and the people step on you and a wild dog sniffs you and you think of poisons and you want to die right there, but instead you just start to cry. And your grief, woman of the living tears, makes a puddle in which you wet your dress as if it were a shroud and, naked, without anyone seeing you, without anyone wanting to see you, you creep into the tomb where, hours later, they will deposit his body: skeletal, bloodied, totally dead.

With your back against the cold stone, your body pale, deathly, you watch him rise up, and you smile. He wears your gray stone around his neck—that is to say, he wears your power, your blood, your strength. The light that floods the tomb when he moves the boulder aside allows you to see him for the last time: beautiful, divine, supernaturally loved.

He looks at you—you are almost sure that he looks

at you—and with your last breath—you are dying—
you say something to him, you call out to him, you
stretch out your hand. The word *love* hangs from the
ceiling like a stalactite. But he continues walking to
meet his fanatic followers, who shout, who throw
themselves onto their knees in the sand, who cover
their faces with their hands.

And he never looks back.

MOURNING

For the first time in her life, Marta sat at the head of the table, and her sister, clean, dressed in white linen and anointed with perfumed oils, sat to her right. She brought out more wine before the carafe was empty, and without saying grace, she devoured the chicken, the fat drumsticks with crispy skin, caramelly, delicious, that had never ever been for her. She looked at María, who looked like a barbarian scraping her teeth against the chicken breast, thigh, wing, and she let out a slow laugh. The laughter of wine and freedom. Laughter that signaled no one else would again stand up from the head of the table and eat the golden fatness of the chicken and behold the beautiful María: her face dirty, her hands greasy, gripping the cup to take a long drink of wine, her mouth overflowing. Wine. A pair of libertine women. She wanted to say to María, Look at us, look at us, how unlike ourselves, so full of pleasure, today, when we should still be in mourning, today, when the house should be shrouded in black. We're alone now, my sister, more than alone—without a man in the house—and you'd think we'd be trembling like kittens that've lost their mother.

But Marta didn't say anything, just smiled. And María returned the smile with teeth covered in pieces of dark meat. They ate their fill and continued eating just to see what would happen, and, their bellies bulging, they went out into the yard with their arms around each other. The night was starry. The animals were asleep, the servants too. The entire world slept a snoring, drunken sleep. They had food, they had water, they had land, they had shelter. Marta could almost smell the sea like on vacation that one time, when their parents were alive, when he wasn't him, but just another one of them: three children running on the beach and returning every now and then, Look Mama a shell, look Papa a crab. Good times, yes—the air smelled like the good days, back when Papa didn't come home bitter, when he didn't lash out at anyone who got in his way with that thin leather switch that quietly ripped open flesh, like it was nothing, until blood sprang up like a red surprise and stung with pain. He started with Mama, moved on to their brother and then to Marta, who managed to protect María from the switch. Papa had turned them into other people, another family. Perhaps that sacred word, *family*, shouldn't even be used. Those days Papa stank, reeked of fermentation, and they hid under the bed while Mama screamed, and sometimes he traded the switch for a whip, which warned them of the coming pain with its *tchas, tchas, tchas* in the air.

Marta hugged her sister María tighter, looking at her childlike face, aged now but so pretty nonetheless, with those strange eyes, so green, so disturbing. She kissed away María's tears and told her that she loved her and asked her sister to forgive her. María knew what she meant. Then María, full of wine and chicken and total freedom, removed her dress and closed her eyes and opened her arms so that her sister could see her whole, naked, crucified. So she could see what a person is capable of doing when there's nothing to stop them. So she would understand from her scars that cruelty would always triumph over helplessness. Someone had written the word *whore* on her stomach with a sharp object, someone had stomped on her right hand until it resembled a flipper, someone had bitten her nipples until they had come loose, flaps of skin hanging from her round breasts, someone had inserted farming tools into her anus and left her hemorrhaging, someone had kicked her until she miscarried, someone, no one, had done anything they wanted for all those days that she lay there unconscious, and the rats, with their eager little teeth, had begun to nibble at her cheeks, her nose, someone, assuredly their brother, had turned her back into wicker from so many lashes. *Tchas, tchas, tchas.*

And infection, scabs, rot, blood, fractures, anemia, venereal disease, pus, pain.

Marta knelt before her sister. She held her arms out to her and she whispered ten, thirty, a hundred times, never again, never again, never again. And Marta was sorry for being healthy, for being a virgin, for being alive. And she sobbed and spit on the ground and cursed their brother. She cursed their brother's grave, cursed his name and cursed his cock and cursed his now-rotting corpse. And hugging her sister's skinny, scabbed knees, she said:

"I have no god but you, María."

Then the back door slammed shut and they both screamed. Damn, the wind. María put her dress back on and they went inside the house, which was suddenly as hostile and cold as a cave. As they approached the table with their candles, they realized that what looked like skin covering the scraps of chicken were dozens of brown cockroaches that started to skitter around, making a crunching sound like rasping leaves. They shrieked as if they'd seen a ghost. Marta said that at times like this—only at times like this—you need a man in the house, and María, who was standing on a chair with her skirts pulled up around her waist, started to laugh like a person possessed, and said no, that she preferred cockroaches, all the cockroaches in the world, over a man in the house. Then she jumped to the floor, and with both of her bare feet, she landed, precisely, on top of two cockroaches, one foot on each, and they popped open like little boxes and released a bright white fluid. Marta told her to quiet down, that someone might hear them, but she also laughed about how something so stupid had made them scream like that and about how her sister wasn't wearing underwear in the middle of the dining room and about how they didn't need a man, much less *that* man, and all the while, she never stopped moving her legs and shaking out her dress in case some bug happened to climb on her, and it looked like she was dancing, and if someone had seen them—one naked from the waist down, all laughs, killing cockroaches, and the other dancing like a lunatic—they would never have thought that three days ago, just three, these women had lost their brother, their only brother.

But that's how it was.

He had been sick awhile, they said it was some illness that he'd caught in the desert. That he'd caught from some woman in the desert, María thought, but she never said it to her sister or to anyone else. She'd witnessed such things: healthy men at death's door in a matter of months, with the black shame, burned like sheaths of rice and blubbering about the devil or the sweet, sweet taste of dates in some imaginary land. María knew that her brother had died from sin, but who would believe her? *She* was the one who bore that cross, not her brother, yes, of course, her perfect brother: pure as holy water. María had a good memory: she remembered the day her brother kicked her out of the house and made her sleep out beyond the servants' quarters and the stables in a dark cowshed with half a roof. His whore sister didn't deserve to sleep on linen or embroidered silk like Marta, the good sister, the pious sister. The whore deserved to sleep with the rats, on a reeking pallet. The whore, the devil's servant, touched herself between her legs and moaned. That's what being a whore meant: taking pleasure in pleasure. He saw her. He went into her room and found María with her hand between her legs. There will be no whores in this house, he said. And that was it. That night he tied her to a water trough and under the beautiful stars he kicked open her face. When Marta came outside to beg him to have mercy on her, he raised his hand and told her that if she took one more step he would kill her. I'll do the same to you, he said, but I'll kill you. Anyone who defends a whore is also a whore, he shouted. And so Marta knelt in the dusty yard watching her brother break their sister with his blows.

Now the two women were alone. Marta had moved into their brother's room, and her old room, exquisite, had gone to María. Now it was time to spoil her, to adore her, to glorify her. Out there in the shed they'd raped her, she who had been a virgin the week before, all the servants took turns, even those who had called her "niña María" the week before. Men, young and old, paraded through. There, on top of her, the town's sexuality came to life and died. There, they abused her and penetrated her anus and her vagina, and he tortured her, he who called himself pure, who called himself a man of God, who was the dear friend of the most holy of holy men, the man who'd been fawned over when he came to the house and who'd had his dusty, calloused feet washed by María with her own divine, exotic perfumed oils.

Marta knew all this because one night she had followed and watched, her eyes shining with fear. And afterward, whenever she closed her eyes, she saw them again and again. Brother on top of sister. María like a dead body, her eyes closed, rocked by the inertia of his movement, like a white corpse—a fly buzzing around her mouth, her eyes, her nostrils—still stained with blood, and him, looking all around like a criminal, stealing back to the main house in the moonlight, his cock stained with the same blood. Did María have her period? Or was she so destroyed that inside she was just an open wound? Neither heaven nor earth was ever the same again. Brother on top of sister, like in the darkest of horrors.

This went on for many, many nights.

The pallet on which her sister lay—half-dead, barely alive—was a filthy heap where maggots bred, and which some men, even though it was free, even though it was easy, found too repulsive. A rotting body, disgusting, stinking. María, sweet beautiful María, her eyes like precious stones from distant mountains, daughter of the sea and the desert, was now too disgusting for the filthiest of strangers. Sometimes, some desperate man would throw a bucket of water on her and just like that, all wet, he'd take care not to touch her too much as he penetrated her quickly, violently, like a goat.

Marta couldn't care for her sister. The walls had eyes and mouths and tongues like serpents. They would tell him immediately and he would do the same to her: he'd put them both, one next to the other, on the same pallet, in the same hell. Marta gave a coin to some maid to take a bucket of water and a sponge to wash her sister's bruised, gray, and bloody body, but she never knew if she actually did it. But she had to have faith. Faith in the maid. Faith that the servant would give her a piece of fish, some bread and milk. Faith that the guard would, for enough money, stop every man in town from using her. At least for those few days of the month. At least on the holy days. At least today. Faith that the messenger boy would give her sister the note telling her to hang on, *the two of us will leave this place soon.* But it was just faith, the most pathetic of feelings. Faith didn't do a goddamn thing. For example, when their brother's friend, the holiest of holy men, visited, he asked after María and her eyes like rare gems, and though excuses were made to deflect his requests, he kept asking after María and her eyes of an otherworldly green, so their brother had no choice but to take him to the filthy shed where he had her bound, half-naked and stained with excrement, spread open in a posture more vile than that of a butchered animal—that man, the holiest of holy men, began to cry and shout and plead and shake their brother, saying, No one can forgive you for what you've done here, untie her right now, you insane, sadistic bastard. But their brother just said, She is a sinner, Father, she is the most sinful of all women. I have seen her. She takes pleasure in the sins of the flesh, Father. I wasn't told this. I had the misfortune of witnessing it, Father, she is repugnant. And if I untie her, Father, then others will think that this can be done without consequences, that it can be this way, and I won't allow it.

And then the man, whose feet María had washed with her own hair, knelt down and prayed for her awhile, a few minutes, and went into the house to have dinner and drinks with the men. As he was leaving, after embracing him, he told their brother: You should untie her. His voice sounded teary, maybe drunk. And their brother, nodding his head a lot, looking down, said, Yes, Father, I will do as you wish. Marta walked out to meet the holy man, and she knelt: Please. It is your brother's house, he responded to Marta, and I can't impose my will upon him, respect for a man is shown through respect for his home, but I have already told him that he should untie her, and I will pray for it to be so. You should have faith, he told Marta before disappearing into the desert, *faith*.

The word tasted like shit on her tongue.

And María remained in the shed.

When their brother got sick, Marta—whom everyone praised for her dedication, her deference, her devotion, her broths, her tenderness, her herbal infusions—cared for him. She fed him, cleaned him, gave him medicine, and even applied a white ointment to his private parts, which burned bright red. But everything that an observer would have interpreted as affection, she carried out with a deep hatred. To the outside eye, Marta was all delicacy, but alone she fed him cold, gelatinous broth, always with a dash of fresh manure, sand, or maggots that she found in the yard and stowed in a box to mix with his food, careful that no one saw. When she washed her brother's body, which had become one huge, bloody, purple wound oozing with pus, she began gently, with warm water, coconut oil, and a sea sponge, but suddenly, without warning, without any changes to her breathing, she became violent. Marta switched the sea sponge for steel wool and scraped his arms up and down like she was sanding wood. She finished her polishing with rubbing alcohol. She was imaginative: she'd pour hot wax or camphor on his wounds, stinging nettle or lemon. Then she'd leave the room and sit on a chair beside the door, her hands crossed in her lap piously, and her eyes closed tight, while inside her brother writhed in pain and made horrific sounds, muted because he could no longer scream: the illness had taken his tongue, and in its place had left a kind of red mush that wiggled around his toothless mouth like some lascivious monster.

Anyone who had seen Marta would have thought she was praying for the health of her sick brother, but she was praying for him to die slowly, as painfully as possible.

And one day he died. It wasn't quick or easy: his gruesome death throes lasted hours. He was thirsty and no one gave him water. Marta closed the doors and windows, and as if it were a show, she sat watching him die. She let him agonize alone, although her brother held out his skeletal hand to her, perhaps begging for company, contact: for her to put her living hand, like a little dove, over his almost-dead hand, for her to wash away his sweat and drip just a few tears onto his forehead, two tiny diamonds, which he might use to pay whatever waited for him on the other side of death. The dying will cry, moan, writhe: they fear that everything they know about heaven and hell is all a lie. Or rather, the truth.

When the man finally went still, his mouth agape and eyes wide as if he'd just heard some hilarious joke, Marta slowly stood up, opened the door, walked through the rooms of the house, went out into the yard, and theatrically threw herself on the ground and screamed and screamed until all the neighbors came. She covered her face with her hands, but there were no tears. She was radiant like a celestial body. María heard her sister's screams, and her heart froze. Then she closed her eyes, crusted over, and opened them again very slowly, like a newborn. And like a newborn, she began to wail, calling to her sister.

Four days later, just four, their brother's friend, the holy man, arrived in town, and then Marta had to pretend, to wail no, no, no, and cry her tearless cry for her dead brother. If only you had been here, she told him because she couldn't think of anything else to say. If only you had been here. But she knew those words were as ridiculous as condolences, as a prayer. What was, was. What is, is. Then the friend, the holy man, asked her to take him to the crypt, and there she left him, kneeling, calling to the dead man like someone calls at the door of a house, as if on the other side of the stone there was still some life left in him to hear.

Marta shrugged her shoulders at such an absurd display and went back to her house, to the party for her liberated sister, to life.

That night, as Marta and María ate lamb, they were startled by a banging on the door. It must be the wind. The wind this time of year, terrible. Marta and María continued eating until they heard the door groan, and raised their heads to watch it swing inward as if pushed by a hand. It opened.

First the flies appeared, and immediately after, their dead brother, shrouded in a nauseating smell. He opened and closed his mouth, as if calling out their names, but no sound fell from that toothless gap, only maggots.

ALI

M iss Ali was strange, strange even in her generosity. She didn't give us, for example, expired food or hand-me-down clothes. She gave us the good stuff. The very same things she ate or wore. I mean, her clothes were too big for us, but she always sent them to the tailor beforehand. And whenever she took a trip, she brought us new clothes, purses, makeup, gifts, as if we were her relatives and not her maids. Miss Ali was just like that. When she made up the grocery list, she asked us what we wanted because, as she told us, there might be something we didn't like, something that didn't agree with us, right? We'd never thought of that. The lady of the house usually ordered whatever she liked, and we had to eat it—that was that. Or, for example, when we went to the supermarket, she gave us her wallet. Just like that: her wallet, in our hands. So she was strange, but good strange. Oh, Miss Ali, you really are good, we'd tell her. Other girls said that the ladies they worked for would give them overripe fruit, suspicious-looking meat, black avocados that were only good for hair, or shoes with a split heel, pants with

a rip in the crotch, lotions that had started to separate. Just crap. All the same: Thank you, miss, yes, very
pretty, very delicious, miss. And the ladies checked
their purses and bags when they left and sometimes
even looked under their skirts in case they'd hidden
some food in their underwear. And they were told: If
you weren't such thieves, we wouldn't have to act like
the police on top of everything else we have to do. The
ladies said this as they groped the girls or patted their
legs over their pants or had them empty their purses
onto the floor.

And the other girls said jealously: So, the fat lady
is really nice, huh? The fat ones are always better. I
hope I find one. These skinny bitches are so miserable. And they're mean. All they think about is how to
get skinnier, and they take pills: Marlene, where are my
pills? I'll bring them to you, miss. What's in those pills?
She walks around like a crazy person, her eyes bugged
out, looking like an owl. Ugh, mine, sometimes when
she has an event coming up, she'll go for days on just
cheese and mineral water, and if you say good morning,
miss—or even if you don't say it—she'll tear your eyes
out! Mine throws up: she orders a large pizza, some
chocolate, potato chips, she shuts her door, eats every
last bite, and then I hear her throwing up again and
again. Poor Karina, the girl who cleans, she's the one
who has to wipe it all up—and no *thank you*, no nothing. No, but they do pay us, don't they? The minimum,
sure, but they pay us. Those ladies' grandparents didn't
even pay their girls; they were their owners, so to speak.
They were taken from the fields—their own mothers

gave them away—and were given a bed and food, and, in return, they said: Thank you, master, may our sweet Lord and Savior bless you and grant you a long life. Sonia worked for one woman who drank and took pills and slept all day, and when she woke up, she'd be furious and smack Sonia silly if she tried to keep her from hitting the kids. When she fired her, oh, how Sonia cried, because Sonia adored those children, and those little ones cried: Don't go, Sonita, don't leave us here all alone, Sonita. And the baby bawled like it was his own mother leaving him—so painful, because Sonia had raised that little boy. Yes, that happened right near here, in the neighboring town with the lake. Somehow her husband had a big important government job, with the mayor. And when the woman was with her friends, everything was all perfect, divine, like a dream. Their little laughs, right? Covering their mouths. Those faces they make: so fake, full of that shit they inject themselves with that makes them look all surprised, more like plastic dolls than women, their eyes all open wide, their lips like frogs. They're all swollen, so ugly, they look like they've been cursed, but they pay a pretty penny to look like that. For parties, they hire white-gloved waiters so they won't get their dark hands all over the white china or the tablecloths that cost more than we earn in a year. And they fill the tables with that pastel-colored raw fish. And they put flowers all over the house. And they bathe in perfume. Must be to hide the smell of vomit. The smell of dirty pajamas and sheets, covered in shit, period blood, farts, from when they don't get up for days on end. No one sees them like that, when you have to go in and whisper, miss? It's mister on the phone, he wants to know if you're up yet. Tell him yes, that I'm in the bathroom. Don't let anyone bother me, Mireya, go with the driver to pick up the children and feed them, and for the love of god, don't let them in here, you understand? And the kids don't even ask for their mom. They did at first, but then they started heading straight to the kitchen on their own. And there they tell you about their day, their soccer game, their tests, their friends, the good and the bad, the things they have in their heads and in their hearts, and you tell them things too, and in the end they're like your own children. They grow up right there in the kitchen: eating with you until they get big, and then it seems weird to them to love you so much, even though deep down they know that you were their mother, and they see you one day in the future, once you've left, and they don't know whether to cry or run into your arms like when they were little and fell down, or to just nod their heads at you because they're now little ladies and little gentlemen of society who know you don't greet the help with hugs and kisses.

The fat lady was a good mother, then?

Yes, Miss Ali was an excellent mother almost to the very end. Then she got her wires crossed and couldn't do it anymore, not anymore. She couldn't even have Mati near her, she couldn't touch him at all. We couldn't believe it, a little thing like that, like baby Jesus, with those golden curls and that little round face, an angel, running to hug her, and Miss Ali with that strange voice, too high, like someone had stepped on a rat, would shout for us to come. As if she were in mortal danger. Of the poor little creature. Her baby. Alicita was already bigger and that girl was always real smart, sharp as a tack. With those big blue eyes that so clearly understood everything. Inhuman, that girl's eyes, like she could see everything inside your head. She must've seen something ugly in her mother because she knew right away. At first sight. She refused to go into whatever room her mother happened to be in. She stopped thinking that she even had a mother: she already saw herself as an orphan, playing by herself and caring for her little brother. It just made your heart break to look at her, so somber, dressing him or telling him to stop crying over silly things, to grow up. And the husband, well, the young man did the best he could with his fat, crazy wife. He went off to work like all the men in the city: at eight o'clock sharp, all in their four-wheel-drive SUVs, all with their shirts and pants ironed by us. And his face, so sad you could die. He already felt like a widower, with his little kids and their insane mother. Once her fits started, her madness, Miss Ali slept in the guest room, and she asked us to bring food to her in bed. She hardly saw her husband anymore. When they did run into each other at home, she told him to go away, and when he tried to hug her, she didn't let him: she let out her shriek like a trampled rat and went back into the guest room, and he stood outside, doing nothing for a long while, sometimes with his hand on the doorknob. The young man made us so sad. All of them made us sad, really. Miss Ali smelled bad, poor thing. Mati didn't sleep well at night. Alicita hardly talked. And the husband, we don't know, he worked until late and just said thank you, thank you.

Whenever Doña Teresa, Miss Ali's mom, came over, things got even worse. She made her bathe, cut her nails, shave, wash all her clothes, air out her room. You could hear the screaming across town. Doña Teresa's driver always came in to help get Miss Ali out of bed, and that man's presence set her off like he was the devil himself. We all ended up scratched and bitten and crying because when Miss Ali saw that man, she freaked out: she turned into a scared bull, two hundred pounds of fury. We practically had to tie her up to get her to the bathroom. When the driver left, Miss Ali seemed to calm down a little, and since *we* understood it, we didn't know how the mother, Doña Teresa, didn't, how she kept bringing the man with her. We'd banned the driver and the gardener and the window washer and the boy who brought the groceries and Alicita's swimming instructor and any other worker from entering the house when Miss Ali was awake because we'd already seen what happened with men. At first, we would ask her: Miss Ali, what's wrong? What's wrong? What happened? When she started having her fits, she sometimes forgot her own name, and she would say, Close the door, lock it, don't sleep with the door unlocked, lock my daughter up, lock her up tight, don't give anyone my daughter's key, lock her up. And she'd check the lock on her bedroom door a hundred times. But her mother didn't ask. May God forgive us, but that lady seemed blind, heartless. She didn't even talk to Miss Ali. She only came because of her leg, and she only asked about her leg, but any idiot could see that her knee was the least of the girl's problems, that silly slip by the pool and the bottles and bottles of painkillers they started giving her, some prescribed by the doctor and others not officially prescribed. In the kitchen, we started talking about looking for other doctors, head doctors, for real lunatics, but who would listen to us girls? Miss Ali was no longer the same person, and every day she became less like herself. It seemed like we were the only ones who saw it. It wasn't her leg—why did they keep talking about her leg? Why did they go on and on about the leg, the leg, the leg? Her leg got better, but she, who was *she*? She was the kind of mom who would watch movies and eat pizza with her kids in bed. They would all draw pictures, sculpt clay, make up their own skits, play dress up. She'd even take us all out for hamburgers. She used to take care of the plants, to eat colorful cereal for breakfast like her kids, to watch Mati sleeping and then say to us, Can you believe I made something so beautiful? She wasn't the woman who ran away from her husband and kids, monstrously fat, stinking, locking and unlocking her door forty times a day. No, that wasn't our Miss Ali. One day, her father, Don Ricardo, came without warning. We let him in, he asked where his daughter was, and we told him she was in the guest room. We were in the kitchen making the coffee he'd asked for when we heard the front door slam shut. We ran to Miss Ali's room, and there she was: her eyes big as saucers, one hand gripping the sheet under her chin, and the other brandishing a pair of nail scissors. She was pointing the scissors at the door, her arm shaking all the way up to her shoulder. Miss? She started to scream. Make him leave, make him leave, make him leave! Who? Your dad? He already left, pretty girl. Make him go. Lock the door, please, don't let him back in. Lock all the doors, don't let him near the girls, don't let him near Alicita, I see him, I see him, and I hear him and I know. What do you know, miss? What do you see? She started to scream that she hurt. What hurts, sweetie? Where? The scissors were still pointing toward the door. But then she did it, fast: she gripped the scissors and she sliced down from her hairline to her jaw. We'd never seen so much blood. Our lady's face cut open like raw beef. Vinicio, Don Ricardo's driver, heard the screams from outside. We put her in the car and took her to the hospital. On the way, we called the husband. Oh, that young man. We waited for news at the house, with the kids. Alicita didn't ask any questions about her mother. We told her she'd had an accident, and she didn't even look at us. Miss Ali came home looking even worse. The bandages on her face looked horrible. She wanted to see for herself and tried to take them off all the time, so they put bandages on her hands too, and took away all the mirrors. We heard from her mother's friends that the doctors said it wasn't good for her to see herself yet, that she had to undergo some treatments first, plastic surgery, because the wound was very ugly, very purple, that she had an infection and it went down her whole face, from her forehead to her neck, that it was a miracle she hadn't lost an eye. We also heard that it had been an accident. That she hadn't known what she was doing. That she had been half-asleep, that she had always been a sleepwalker, since she was a little girl, a sleepwalker! No one asked us what happened, because if anyone had asked, we would have told them that she took the scissors and stabbed them into her skin and dragged them down like she wanted to destroy her face, that she was alert, lucid, that her father had just been in her room and that she was terrified of him, that she asked us to keep the girl away from him, and that he was the one she actually wanted to stab with the scissors. But everyone talked instead about sleepwalking, and us girls' opinions didn't matter, so we went about feeding Miss Ali through a straw and fluffing her pillows and making sure she was comfortable and calm. We took care of the children and the young man, who was like a lost soul. We watered the plants for Miss Ali, we cuddled little Alicita, her heart a little colder every day, we answered the telephone and said, Yes, miss, okay, no, she's asleep right now, yes, Doña Teresa, she's better today, yes, she had carrot puree for lunch, yes, sir, yes, don't worry, we're here, it's nothing, goodbye, yes, miss, I'll give her the message. When the mother, Doña Teresa, came, Miss Ali turned to face the wall, and she sometimes stayed that way the entire afternoon. The woman brought her friends with her to keep from getting bored, even though it was clear that her daughter didn't like people to come: she hid her head under the sheets and stayed there, like she was wearing a shroud. We were constantly serving coffee, glasses of water, diet sodas, and cookies; we had to order desserts from the café in the mall. Doña Teresa's friends might have thought they were being nice by visiting

Miss Ali and yakking and gossiping about everyone, but we went in sometimes and we saw her there, immobile, miserable, like a chained animal, and sometimes she had streaks of tears where the bandages didn't cover her face. When all those ladies left, what a relief, we had to air out the whole house from all the hair spray and perfume. We were like tadpoles trying to breathe, opening and closing our mouths. Finally the house emptied itself of a thick liquid, as if it were a fish tank with strange fish in it: all painted nails and styled hair and gold accessories. They left. We went back to being like before. Miss Ali came out from under the sheets and asked for the dessert they'd left behind. We laughed and ate the desserts, and we had our Miss Ali back for a minute until she grabbed our hands and said, terrified: Does the lock on the door work? And to Alicita's room? And we said yes, of course they worked, and we patted her greasy hair, and she asked us to take care of her, and she fell asleep until her first nightmare came. In her nightmares they were trying to undress her. In her nightmares someone made her do things she didn't want to do. In her nightmares she locked all the doors. In her nightmares there was always an adult with a set of keys.

Around that time, the young man took the children to his mother's because something happened with Miss Ali and Alicita. The truth is, we still believe she wouldn't have done anything bad, that she just wanted to help her daughter, to teach her, but the young man walked in when Miss Ali was in the bath with her naked little daughter and that plastic thing that was like a big cock, and the man went crazy, he shouted at her and hit her, he called her a crazy bitch, what are you doing, you fat crazy bitch, you stupid filthy bitch, I'm going to lock you away, and she just cried. That's what the girls from next door said they heard, because we weren't there. It was Sunday. So the young man took the kids in their pajamas, in the middle of the night, to his mother's house. After that, Miss Ali couldn't even lift her head. Doña Teresa came to stay, and Miss Ali didn't say a word around her. When we were alone, she sometimes opened her eyes and asked about Alicita. We told her she was fine and she asked to see her. Then she'd start to cry and the mother would send us to get her pills. A doctor friend of Doña Teresa's had given her some pills that left her drooling and staring off into space. We thought it would be better for her to cry because it seemed like Miss Ali had a lot to cry over, a lifetime's worth, but the mother gave her those pills like they were candy. All the time. It made us sad to see her like that, turned into such a monster. That scar crisscrossing her face like a purple worm, her tremendous size, her drool, her lost eyes, the white bathrobes that her mother had brought from the United States so she'd always look clean. Days passed. And months. Christmas came. Yes, that was the worst part: Christmas. Miss Ali seemed a little better, she stood up, went down to the kitchen, had cereal for breakfast, and told us that she wanted to buy Christmas presents, so we imagined she wanted to get her kids back, her husband. We were so happy, and we left her alone for a little while to get dressed to go to the mall. When we returned, she had gone into the bathroom and locked the door. We heard a lot of water running, for too long. Miss Ali? We knocked on the door. Miss? We went to find the keys, and when we got back, there she was, wrapped in a towel, her hair soaked, long and straight, stuck to her back. She smiled at us. What's wrong?

The mall was a madhouse: Christmas carolers, screaming children, and hundreds of people. We were worried—Miss Ali hadn't been out of the house in months—but besides a slight limp and her weight, no one would've known there was anything strange about the woman, that she had been through what she'd been through. That's the way it is, isn't it? You see people, and you have no idea what goes on inside the walls of their home. Almost immediately, she looked at us and said she had to buy some important gifts for some important people, and that those people couldn't see those gifts, so we had to separate for a little while. Everything seemed to be going well. She winked and smiled at us, walked off with her purse, in her tracksuit, her red running shoes. She looked like a normal girl, the same Miss Ali as always, who was going up to the fifth floor to buy us who knew what. We watched her go up the elevator—Christmas music was playing, and it seemed like she was her old self again, that she was going to be a mother to her children and a wife to her husband, and we thought that it was a miracle from Baby Jesus because we had prayed so much and they say that God actually listens to poor people because he loves them more, so the misery of poverty had to be good for something, to help us get Miss Ali back, to end her nightmare and everyone else's. We saw her peek over the balcony of the fifth-floor café, and then we knew, immediately we knew—there's something that tells you, something unexplainable—that something terrible was about to happen. Several simultaneous screams, then the sound of a body being annihilated, like a sack of glass, stone, and raw flesh, one side of Miss Ali's skull smashed, melted, and more screaming, a scream that comes from inside you, a scream like a stab, a scream from the heart and lungs and stomach, and Miss Ali lying there, like a huge doll with her legs splayed, an inhuman position, like she was filled with stuffing instead of bones. We stood there, frozen, our hands over our mouths, until the doctors came, the police, the husband, Doña Teresa, Don Ricardo, and someone started shaking us, telling us to go home and take care of all the people who immediately started to arrive, desperate to know why, how, and Doña Teresa, clutching a handkerchief, said *accident*, terrible accident, wet floor, she was unstable, you know, her knee, but she insisted on going to the mall because she was a wonderful mother, of course, of course, her friends said, and she wanted to buy Christmas presents for the kids. What a nightmare, yes, an accident, our poor, sweet girl, the friends said. But when the lady left the room, one of them took out her phone and read the news about the "Shopping Mall Suicide" while the others listened, their ring-covered hands over their mouths, their eyes wide, unblinking. Another lady said quietly that she'd heard strange things about the family, things between the brother and the sister, between the father and the daughter. The others angrily shut her up: Don't repeat stupid things.

At the burial, a woman at the cemetery handed out white roses so that Miss Ali's loved ones could place them on her coffin. When she walked by, she skipped us and gave roses to some very elegant ladies wearing big black sunglasses who we'd never seen before. The day after the burial, Don Ricardo gave us each a hundred dollars, for the days we worked that month, he told us, and before we left, Doña Teresa checked our purses and bags in case we had stolen anything. There, where she didn't check us, we had Miss Ali's wedding ring, her pretty watch, and a pearl necklace she'd never worn. Doña Teresa didn't say goodbye, nor thank you. Behind her, Alicita watched us with those huge, intelligent, frightened blue eyes. The exact same eyes as her mother.

CORO

There's a time for talk and a time for action. These women had renounced the latter long ago. Gossip floats like a ghost through the spacious rooms. Carpeting is no longer in fashion, so the porcelain tiles reflect watches, embroidered bags, French manicures, and teeth that, from so many smiles, seem threatening. Air kisses, flattery, air kisses, flattery. A glance up and down at someone who has gained weight, aged, chosen their outfit poorly: it is usually the same person. María del Pilar's—Pili's—new house is everything you'd expect from her: enormous, climate-controlled, monochromatic, expensive. Maybe a little bigger, but about the same as the other women's houses. Even so, they're given a tour, a conga line of compliments through rooms that smell like paint, like brand-new. The bed linens, white percale, gray pinstripes, all of it purchased in the United States; the walk-in closet straight out of a catalog; the hilarity that the bathroom, gigantic, has two mirrors, two sinks, two toilets, two tubs.

"Have you had it blessed yet?"

The question does not amuse María del Pilar, Pili,

who thinks that this is the moment for effervescent praise, *her* moment, so she turns to Verónica and she tells her very slowly no, not yet, and a smile remains frozen on her mouth, as if it had been drawn on top of an unhappy expression. Verónica says that an unblessed house is like an unbaptized baby: more vulnerable to the evil eye. She realizes that the other women are looking at her with contempt, and she backtracks: "I don't believe in those things, you know, but that's what they say." She shifts her voice, making *things* sound like *thangs* and *you* like *ya*, pretending like she's from the streets. Everyone laughs, they mock her, they imitate Verónica's imitations: Well then, according to Verónica, you should tie a bundle of aloe leaves with red ribbon and hang it over the door. And a horseshoe. Yes, and a Chinese mirror next to it to ward off bad spirits. And burn palo santo to purify the space. And sweep outward. And elephants. And white candles. And spit aguardiente on the floor. And place a Buddha in a saucer of water. And an altar with candles in the entryway. And burn incense—*insaynse*. And tie a stone around your wrist with red ribbon, or Verónica will give you the evil eye, can't you see she's half witch? She's a witch, and she's half.

Verónica laughs too. Nothing has changed since high school: the darkest one, of more foreign or more dubious descent, the daughter of divorced parents, who had to share a room with her sister; the one who is decidedly different, who has to earn her place at the table. Something of a class clown, a minion, a scavenger. It's crucial that she make them laugh by using the language of the lower classes, and that she include herself within this lower class: that she be humbler, that she be willing to do them favors—like some type of chore if there isn't enough help around the house—and that, most importantly, she be the one to offer up their next victim. Yes, she must utter the first and last name, state how, where, and with whom. That is to say, she must wet her hands and face with blood as she skins and guts the kill, the acquaintance, the friend who isn't present, so that the others may stab at her with toothpicks, their pinkies in the air, savoring the raw, delicious gossip.

Their disdain is actually fear in disguise, a bit of operetta, but they don't realize it. They rip apart anyone who's been unfaithful, who's had a child outside of marriage, who's in the closet, who's had fresh plastic surgery, who's got a bankrupt husband, who's gained an extreme amount of weight, and they don't let them loose until they've been bled dry, empty, nothing but fur on the tiles, then they dab at their maws with fine linen. They throw their prey on the pile of bodies that exists in each of their climate-controlled living rooms. Then they move on to the next. This is what they call coffee, a housewarming, a birthday, a pool party, a funeral. This is what they call a get-together.

They don't see themselves, but if they could, if it were possible to leave their bodies so that they could really see themselves, seated on those bright white sofas, surrounded by so much luxury, devouring a woman who they greet warmly at the supermarket, their husband's best friend, their child's badly behaved classmate, then they'd cut out their tongues—they'd have to—and then lay them out to dry like cocoa beans and wear them around their throats: a necklace, a reminder of their own rottenness. But things stay the same. People are incapable of seeing themselves, and that is the root of all evil.

Verónica had only been accepted into the group conditionally: the one wearing long sleeves to cover her very hairy, very dark arms, the one who went to her grandparents' house for summer vacation and not to a camp ten thousand miles away to learn French, the one who sometimes repeated outfits—and they'd see her in photos wearing the same dress to several different parties and not say a word, but they knew that the only purpose served by keeping such a person around was their own entertainment. But tonight is difficult because it's been a few months since the fat girl's suicide at the mall, and there's nothing new to discuss, so after a quick recap—their classmate's pregnancy and the baby's father, that they'd been lovers for years, and the poor wife, but also what a moron, the whole world knew, it was the talk of the town—they all start to get nervous and look up at the ceiling because not talking about others means having to talk about themselves, and after the tour of the entire house—including the backyard and the pool area, complimenting each other's skin, hair, sandals, the beautiful necklaces that someone's niece makes, the smoked salmon tartlets—there's not much left to say of what can be said.

Someone has to break the silence, the silence that might last only a few seconds but that they choke on like an ocean forced down their throats. Something that they shouldn't talk about—and everyone has something—could escape. Also, silence isn't good because it leaves space for thinking about how being together, an afternoon with friends, consists of carving up and dismembering other people, impaling them to examine their faults, and about how this same search for the next victim is being repeated behind dozens of gigantic double doors made of walnut or plated steel. They are exactly the same. There are other women, in other living rooms, maybe thinking about *your* past, about you. There are other women with your name in their mouths.

Nativity Corozo—Coro, as she was christened by who knows which employer who knows how long ago because they didn't like the name Nativity, and because *she's mine, dammit, I can call her whatever I want*—enters the room with the discretion of a lizard, incongruous for a woman of her size, her breadth. An incongruence of nature only explained by the years and years of domestic work that function like Chinese foot-binding, atrophying, breaking, creating deformities as strange as a grand woman like Nativity Corozo becoming invisible. She approaches María del Pilar and says something in her ear. Pili huffs with impatience and asks for her purse. Then she excuses herself to her friends: My husband didn't have time to pay her, obviously, he rushed out so fast, thinking about so many other things, and Coro has to leave right now for some reason. Sorry, girls, maid problems. Coro returns. An African deity dressed in a poorly designed white uniform made of rough fabric, open at the chest and close to bursting at her hips and butt, bunched up all around her waist. The only thing no employer has been able to take from her in over thirty years of domestic service is the red scarf she wears on her head. She uses a threat veiled as something helpful: Oh, miss, it's just that my hair falls out sometimes when I'm cooking, and if I don't wear the scarf, those black hairs of mine will fall right into the pot. But of course Coro's hair does not fall out.

María del Pilar doesn't have change and everyone rummages in their purses to try and break the bill for her. In the end they can't, everyone has the same large bills and they think it's funny, fucking hilarious actually, and Coro goes home to spend her one free weekend with half her salary and a *go now* and a *thank you, miss*.

When Coro leaves, everyone talks about her: Isn't it strange to have a woman so, how do we put it, *black*, working in the house, doesn't it smell different because they smell different, and how sweet she is with her scarf like Aunt Jemima's, the black lady on the syrup label when we have pancakes, and how modern of María del Pilar to let her staff use accessories, but it looks good on her, *exotic*, and how much do you pay her, and oh, what a deal, I pay mine more, oh, I've been cheated, maybe so, and now they say we should give them benefits—paid time off, sick leave, all that—and I say, I don't say we *shouldn't*, because they're human beings, but how, how can we pay for all that? It's enough already. Yes. It's a lot. And now they want us to bend over and massage their feet! And coffee breaks. No, impossible, what? We have to work to pay the housekeeper? It's not fair, if a person has a housekeeper it's because they need her, and I treat mine so well, I give her clothes, clothes for her kids, food, a room, toiletries, basically everything— and who gives *me* things? No one! No one gives me a thing, and I'm just giving, giving, giving. Right, we also hire one person for each job, it's not like we make them do *all* the work, we're humane, I have one girl who comes in to iron and another girl who takes care of the kids. So spoiled, these women, I mean look at yours, you even give her a pretty uniform, but she's so fat it's ripping at the seams.

The motion-sensor light on the patio blinks on and off as someone repeats the story of someone or other who caught one of her maids taking a nap and threw a glass of water in her face and the girl didn't even wake up, she just turned over and asked for five more minutes. That outdoor light is so annoying, it's so sensitive that it practically turns on for anything, and since there are so many bugs and animals around here on all this land, it flashes all the time, you can't even sleep. We all have the same problem, it's terrible. The light turns off and then blinks right back on again. It happens seven times, they have to go out to see what's going on. All the women go outside, laughing from the cocktails and the adven- ture: going out onto the patio to see what's tripping the motion sensor. María del Pilar grabs the pool net like a lance. It's all too funny: the platform sandals, the white linen outfit, her hands covered in rings, the net held like a weapon. Someone takes a picture. Creeping along, a strange snout, pointy, hides in the grass. It's a rat. It's a snake. It's an iguana. Rat. Iguana. Snake. María del Pilar, ready to behead any living creature with the pool net, shakes the bushes so that the animal will run out, but nothing does. How boring. Suddenly, something moves. Huntresses, they follow. Seen from high above, the line of ladies would look like a procession of blond ants. The creature has scurried into the maid's room. They all follow behind.

First, the smell—like heavily used coins, like mildew, old hides tanning, something turned sour, something wet stored in a closet in the tropics. The room is a closet. There are no windows and it's as wide as a bus. The toilet is so close to the bed, separated by only a shower curtain with hearts on it, that someone shitting and someone sleeping could hold hands. A calendar with a photo of baby chicks on the left wall and a frameless mirror on the right. A bare bulb hangs from the ceiling. This wasn't supposed to be part of the tour, but the excitement has turned them into children, and without discussing it, they decide to be what they usually avoid being: different. They open drawers and put on Coro's clothes, Nativity Corozo's clothes, over their own. One of them sticks pillows inside her pants and dances around shaking her new ass, and another one picks up a red shirt and puts it over her head like a scarf. They take photos imitating Coro. This one rubs her lips together, the one over there pretends to sweep the floor, another to clean the mirror, and the one with the prosthetic ass imitates a black woman, how she thinks a black woman acts: demanding her entire salary with her hands on her hips because she's going away for the weekend to dance wildly and eat coconut. It's all hilarious.

A big furry bug, something like a tarantula, falls to the floor. Everyone rushes out of the room, screaming, pushing, frightened drunk girls, smiling. They take off Coro's dresses, Nativity Corozo's dresses, throw them on the ground, into the pool, and why not, they throw Verónica in too, who has been waiting outside, her arms crossed, because she didn't want to participate or because she wanted to stand watch. Their laughter is now a wild howling. Verónica comes up for air and one of them dunks her head back under. They're not drowning her, it's just for fun. The light, with its red, eyelike sensors, blinks on and off nonstop. Their hands project moving shadows: monsters swimming in the pool. A tropical rhythm plays somewhere in the distance—they must be having a party at the club not too far off. Everything seems to amplify the general atmosphere of depravity. From the bottom of the pool, Verónica sees the same snout as before, that sharp black snout, swim into the filter. Every time she tries to come up for air, someone pushes her head back down.

María del Pilar, with the pool net, goes back into the servants' quarters and starts savagely smashing the bug on the floor. The light bulb, which she's hit, dances right to left and left to right. The creature might've already been dead, but after thirty blows it definitely is now. As she kills it, she thinks about how it's the first time she's ever done this—killed—that her father always took care of these things, or her maid, or her husband. But her father is dead, her maid is gone for the weekend, and her husband is who knows where with she *does* know who. But no matter who you are, killing is nothing—all you need is the will to do it. Scenes of her husband seated, his legs open, with that woman sucking his cock, that sound, the desperate sloshing of fellatio, mixed with the smell of dust, hot wax, and rotten citrus, with the image of the baby chicks on the calendar, with her own face—red, wild, disfigured by rage—in the frameless mirror.

Outside, the girls play. Verónica tries to swim away, but they surround her, so many of them, from every corner of the pool. Come on, she's yours, watch out over there, don't let her get by you. The automatic light, blinding, like in an interrogation room, turns on and off, turns off and on, making a metallic click, and between that and the splashing, they can barely hear Verónica's cries that seem to say, That's enough, girls, enough for real.

María del Pilar has shattered the light bulb with the pool net, so she uses the glow of her phone to locate the dead spider. She screams just as someone shoves Verónica's head back underwater. Everyone runs to find María del Pilar, horrified, looking at something in her hand: it's a little doll made of blond hair, *her* blond hair, tied with red ribbons, her name written on them. They make her throw it into the toilet and flush. They hug her, they console her, they say it's superstition, lies, don't buy into it, don't be silly, it's all a bunch of servants' nonsense. And María del Pilar sobs and screams because she looked at her doll and her doll looked back at her.

"That's ridiculous, Pili."

They all go outside. They're going to head back into

the house, they're going to have another cocktail and laugh about this.

The light snaps back on like a guillotine. On the surface of the water, her arms and legs spread open, Verónica's body floats adrift.

BLEACH

Crickets, dried leaves, toads, scraps of paper, plastic bags, candy-bar wrappers, cigarette butts, water bugs, heron shit, bats, flowers, more dried leaves. Sometimes a dead iguana, floating faceup like on a little invisible crucifix. They fish. They fish. From time to time they raise their heads and see a boat and real fishermen moving through the real water—raw water, free, undomesticated—to pull out fish, not shit. This thought doesn't cross their minds. The river takes in everything: grayish brown, filthy. The pool, on the other hand, is a mink stole in the middle of a quagmire. Useless. Sullied with a disgraceful ease. They haven't finished fishing out the last dead bug when another dry leaf falls in. Dirty. It never stops being dirty. They have to add bleach every day. Bleach that comes from the United States and disinfects the water better than the local brand. Three cups of bleach. The cup filled to the rim. They reminded them twenty times and hung three signs in the supply closet:

For the pool: three cups of bleach *to the rim*.

Underneath *rim*, someone had drawn a dick. On all

three signs. At this job, you can't think. Thinking would be to invite insanity. You have to work and work, even though it's impossible to clean this pool with its turquoise waters that will never, ever be perfectly clean. You turn around for one second, and there's a cricket, a flower, a cigarette butt, a scrap of paper, a bee. Sometimes a dead bird, one of those yellow ones that fly in pairs, one little bird with its wings splayed in the water and the other hopping on the side of the pool: nature left wanting.

There are three men who clean the pool area. They wear white uniforms that their wives wash by hand with the local bleach, and they turn grayish, tarnished, no matter how hard they scrub, their knuckles raw, no matter how long they hang them in the sun to whiten them. So they receive new uniforms, blinding, that are taken out of their paychecks. The pool always has to look like a mirror, even though in all this time no one has ever swum in it. From the hotel windows, the tourists see the river and the pool—the latter, a little blue eye that the three men have dedicated hours upon hours of their lives to. In vain.

Crickets, dry leaves, candy wrappers.

That's what vacations in these countries are all about: contrasts. For breakfast, there's passion-fruit juice on a table crowned with crisp, heavenly white linen, served on the terrace of a perfect suite with an enormous bed and cloud-like comforters, and she can gaze languidly at the river, that never-ending train of water. She knows these countries are dirty, she saw it on the way in: the muddy buses, the face of the little girl who asked for spare change and whose gaze she couldn't avoid in spite of her sunglasses, the dusty, almost sepia clothes of the people waiting to cross at the light, the stagnant water pooling in potholes, on the sidewalks. But here and now, who would know it? The bathrobe with the hotel's golden logo feels like a polar bear's thick, downy fur, rinsed in arctic water. From inside its embrace, you can believe the fantasy that all is right in the world. It's impossible to think of life's endless misfortunes when you're immersed in a bath of such pure water, when the towels, warm snow, are stuffed animals perfumed with eucalyptus, when the tub looks brand-new and the mirror only reflects beautiful surfaces, immaculate, dazzling. Pills become unnecessary because everything is as it should be: clean smelling, pleasant. Your foot sinks from view into the carpet, soft as puppies, so fleecy and smooth that it makes you want to cry. Opening your suitcase—don't do it—would only bring in the filth of the outside world, with its underwear, its pajama pants, its books, its plastic toiletry kit with half-used deodorant, under-eye concealer, sunscreen, assorted antiaging creams, lip gloss, vibrator: none of that has a place here. Even the phone charger, like a long black intestine, would look horrific against such an immaculate wall. No. This is a new world, it is absolution.

She looks at herself in the mirror for a second and covers the reflection of her face with her hand. She shouldn't have used that self-tanner. She feels stained, unworthy of the world that surrounds her. She remembers how her skin had been the color of mother-of-pearl, her face carved from pure alabaster, and now it's a pinkish cardboard carrot. The feeling of ridiculousness is so great she's nauseated by it. How can a person survive without luxury? This is what loneliness feels like. Beauty had been her company: her cape of invulnerability, her guarantee of intimacy. Nothing could resist it. That's what being beautiful is: no one tells you no.

On the terrace, she puts a crunchy starched napkin on her lap; the robe opens a little, her thighs peek out, her dyed legs, loose like jellyfish, the little green veins that have traced roads for a while now—odious highways from her groin to her feet. She is nothing like the women in the magazines, in the movies, so uncorrupted, such iridescent, pearly women. Is she still a woman? The star-shaped fruits on her plate glow underneath the white sunshade beside the silvery reflections from the teapot. The round sesame-seed rolls, the milk falling in ribbons into the tea, the butter shaved into curls, the plump, buxom strawberries, bloodred—it's all morbid. She opens her robe all the way and lets the sun douse her like a garden hose. It's too late now for any other touch. The man who brought her breakfast smiled, he smiled a lot. A dark man dressed like a little soldier from a children's play. A dark man making a tiny bow. But he'd called her *madame* the way you call a grandmother *madame*, and she saw not even a thread of desire in his eyes until she pulled out his tip. She is already invisible, even to these men, the last living hope of her beauty: the foreign woman, as unprecedented in these parts as snow, a precious object of the other's desire. Or rather, that's what she was up until she doesn't exactly know when, but what she is no longer, and, of course, will never be again. She remembers a lover with chocolate skin in one of these countries—his firm ass, his back like dark wood, his hair full of childlike ringlets, on a pure white bed in a hotel just like this one. She remembers the happy abandon of touching the suede surface of the man. She remembers, also, his ferocious pummeling on all fours, a kiss from thick lips, a tongue the flavor of Coca-Cola. She opens her legs slightly and touches herself. She's dry inside and out. A calla lily abandoned in a vase without water, all crumpled folds and gray pistil, stamens emptied of all pollen. She looks at the tray, so symmetrical, the fresh rosebuds that they've brought her in a silver vase, long like a tube, the little white plates with butter and jam, the exquisite china for the tea. She searches for any wetness and sticks her middle finger into the butter, but stops when she gets to her belly button. She thinks of sucking it, but she wipes it clean with a linen napkin that, just like that, is no longer immaculate. She is disgusted by the now-greasy napkin and can think of nothing other than its dirtiness, violated. She throws it over the balcony and watches it glide downward to land in the pool. She indulges in a forbidden fantasy: a child, a boy or a girl, in her arms, hugging her neck, pointing to a falling napkin and saying, Look, Mama, a seagull, a seagull. She indulges in a forbidden fantasy: the man with chocolate skin appears with a cup in his hand, he rubs the back of her neck and watches the river with her as he takes his first sip of coffee.

While in one of those white hotel suites, it's best not to fantasize about what never was or to stare thirty floors down, to where the world begins, at those three poor men who, instead of taking the glass elevator to her room to love her desperately, for the last time, to devour hunks of her still-alive flesh, are down there, cleaning a pool that will never be clean. She would happily give in to their cannibalism, to those three men who now, most certainly, look at her with an asexual lust, a lust for only what she has in her purse. She would give them everything for one embrace. It should be forbidden to look at things that make you feel this way. The uselessness of certain actions and certain lives. Three men cleaning a pool for other people when, every day, at all hours, there will always be more stains, shit, litter, crucified iguanas. A foreign woman who sets her china teacup on its saucer, her robe floating like a white bat behind her, the river in the background, that train of water that will outlast everything. And below, three men who will make sure, like they do every day, that the pool is once again immaculate.

OTHER

Since it's the fifteenth—payday—the lines stretch almost all the way back to the produce section. You look for a less crowded register, but a lot of people are doing the same thing, and it's no use: you'll have to wait.

There are so many people in the supermarket that they've run out of magazines to flip through, and the only thing left to look at is the ceiling, your nails, the other women's carts, and you think to yourself: *For a country that's going bankrupt, it's nice people can still buy three kinds of American cereal.* And finally, half-dead from boredom and wanting to murder the crazy woman buying mountains of toilet paper, you look into your own cart to make sure you didn't forget anything. It's a ridiculous exercise because if something's missing, too bad: if you leave, you lose your spot. You've never been able to do what other people do, hold up the line because you forgot something, whether it be milk or fabric softener.

The first thing you see are the sardines: red tins stamped with grayish-blue fish that look very happy, but surely aren't. *Did I get enough?* you ask yourself. He likes to eat sardines with yucca and onion at least once a week. *Why does he love sardines so much?* you wonder as you give in, glance around, and slowly open a bag of potato chips. That act of rebellion, eating things in the supermarket before paying for them, is one of the few you allow yourself.

It's the only one you allow yourself.

Why does he love those fucking sardines? you think. *They're like aluminum foil, with those little bones that scratch the roof of your mouth. They taste like salty mud.*

The children can't stand them either, but he loves them, he demands them, and so you always get four tins a month, even though he is the only one who's going to eat them, even though you'll have to cook something different for yourself and the kids.

Beside the sardine tins, the artichokes peek out like hand grenades. *Abominations. Why does he like them? They're expensive, hard to eat, and almost tasteless.* You have to steam them for him and serve them with a sauce made of cheese, Tabasco, and mustard, and once he finishes nibbling the tips of the leaves—*like a big fag,* you think—you have to pick up his plate, get rid of the hairy parts—*like a gringa's pussy, disgusting*—and come back to the table with the hearts cut up and covered in sauce.

He eats the hearts with his hands.

You stare at the beers. He's capable of smacking the kids if he gets home from work and doesn't find his can of beer and frozen mug waiting for him. Everything just how he likes it. As much as you try, you can't cure the children of their obsession with that mug: they're fascinated by the water inside it and the little colorful fish floating around. One day he found Junior drinking out of it and shaking it to make the fish move. He made his head swivel with a slap, and his orange juice flew all over the room. That wasn't a toy. It was *his* beer mug, and the next time he saw Junior with it, he'd burn his fingers with matches.

"I'm going to burn your hand if you ever touch my mug again," he said, picking up a piece of paper and holding it over the flame of a lighter. "Like this."

You have to wash the mug and keep it in the freezer until he walks in the door at 5:45 p.m. Not a moment sooner. Not a moment later. You have to take it out, open the beer, and serve it, tilting the cup and the can so that there isn't too much foam. Nor too little. He's capable of calling you a moron, a retard, a bitch if you don't do it right.

"You idiot, you ruined my beer. I know you did it on purpose, you're always trying to fuck me over."

There is also *his* yogurt. The vanilla yogurt with strawberry jam at the bottom. He takes them and puts them in the freezer of *his* refrigerator, as he calls it. Every night he eats one while he watches television lying in *his* recliner. He counts them, the yogurts, he counts them, so when the kids, who love sweets, eat one, you have to say it was you and endure his tirade without looking up until he exhausts himself, because, oh, if you look up—

"Are you challenging me, huh? Are you fucking challenging me, you piece of shit?"

Sometimes he makes you go to the store, no matter what time it is. Even if it's raining. It's your punishment: you've taken what isn't yours. Worse: you've taken what is *his*.

You keep looking at the cart. You don't have the cereal the kids asked for, and you feel bad. If you got that cereal, you wouldn't have enough money for the steak, and he likes his fillets without any gristle, without any fat. He likes expensive fillets even though he won't let go of one red cent for the rest of the month after buying them. So you grabbed three boxes of off-brand cereal instead, one for each child, and the worst brand of pads, the scratchy ones, the ones that come apart right away and cover your panties in little balls of fluff.

But you have the flank steak and the peanuts to make him his guata, the Coffee-Mate he takes to the office, the Kleenex for his car, his *Stadium* magazine, the fried beans for watching the game, the passion fruit for his juice. Passion fruit: with its snot-like texture, you don't understand how anyone could like it.

Once again, you've bought the discount shampoo, the one that's like washing with dish soap. The one that makes your hair look nice is the other one, the one you never buy.

As you are lost in thought, the line moves forward: the woman in front of you takes the last things out of her cart. This woman is buying the shampoo for color-treated hair that every month you say you're going to buy for yourself. She doesn't have any sardines. She doesn't have artichokes.

She looks at you, smiles, and sets the little divider across the conveyor belt, that little metal barrier that separates her purchases from yours. Her shampoo from yours. Her choices from yours.

Someone returns an empty cart. You put it beside your full one. You transfer to this other cart the sardines, the beers, the guata ingredients, the beans, the fucking artichokes, the shitty yogurts, the goddamn Coffee-Mate, the snotty passion fruit, and the copy of *Stadium*, with all its asshole Barcelona and Emelec players, each one worse than the last.

"Are you getting that?" the cashier asks, pointing to the other cart.

You look at her.

"Ma'am, are you going to get that?" the cashier repeats, jutting her chin at the cart with the shining tins of sardines.

You shake your head.

She calls over a boy to return everything to the shelves. You look at him out of the corner of your eye. He looks at you. You nod for him to take it all back. And, smiling, you say some words to yourself that no one else can hear.

More Translated Literature
from the Feminist Press

Arid Dreams: Stories by Duanwad Pimwana,
translated by Mui Poopoksakul

August by Romina Paula,
translated by Jennifer Croft

La Bastarda by Trifonia Melibea Obono,
translated by Lawrence Schimel

Beijing Comrades by Bei Tong,
translated by Scott E. Myers

The Iliac Crest by Cristina Rivera Garza,
translated by Sarah Booker

The Living Days by Ananda Devi,
translated by Jeffrey Zuckerman

Mars: Stories by Asja Bakić,
translated by Jennifer Zoble

The Naked Woman by Armonía Somers,
translated by Kit Maude

Pretty Things by Virginie Despentes,
translated by Emma Ramadan

The Restless by Gerty Dambury,
translated by Judith G. Miller

**Testo Junkie: Sex, Drugs, and Biopolitics in the
Pharmacopornographic Era** by Paul B. Preciado,
translated by Bruce Benderson

Women Without Men by Shahrnush Parsipur,
translated by Faridoun Farrokh